U0085000

序　言

今日護士的任務，已擴及帮助病患維持健康，與指導健康教育的範圍。對病人真誠的關心，與經常表露體貼、親切的態度，是中外護士共同的自我期許，也是病患及其家屬、親友對白衣天使的期盼。無論身處海外，或在國內的外國醫院工作，若因為語言的隔閡，而無法讓外國病患感受到關切之情及溫馨的服務，總是一大遺憾。

我們編撰這本「**護士英語會話**」，就是要帮助您達到英語會話流利順暢的目的。每章均根據各種護理實況，編輯成實用、易於了解的醫療會話。您可以利用簡潔明瞭的對話，很快學會如何用英文指導孕婦、小兒科病童、糖尿病患者、外科手術病人、乃至於動不動就使用命令語氣的病患等，完成他們所需要的治療；內容方面則著眼於臨床的說明、指導等重要工作，完全符合實際應用的需要。

為加速學習效果，特闢下列專欄：「護士必背英語句型」，可以依實際情況，因人、因時、因地之不同而舉一反三；「字彙備忘欄」可以增進您護理專業字彙的數量，是您活用會話的墊脚石；此外，由於護理方面的溝通上，除了利用語言表達外，表情、態度及氣氛也非常重要，因此於章末加上「護理重點」，予以解說。

本書經過多次審慎編校，若有不足之處，望各界不吝指教，隨時批評斧正。

編者　謹識

Editorial Staff

● 企劃・編著／卓美玲

● 英文撰稿

Bruce S. Stewart・Edward C. Yulo

● 校訂

劉　毅・陳怡平・陳威如・王慶銘
林順隆・林佩汀・陳瑠琍・王蓁蓁
劉瑞芬・許文美

● 校閱

Bruce S. Stewart・Lois M. Findler
John H. Voelker・Keith Gaunt

● 封面設計／曹馨元

● 版面設計／張鳳儀・林惠貞

● 版面構成／蘇淑玲

● 打字

黃淑貞・倪秀梅・蘇淑玲・吳秋香

目錄

本書採用米色宏康護眼印書紙，版面清晰自然，不傷眼睛。

LESSON 1

對住院病患作自我介紹及病房簡介

Introduction, General Explanation on Admission

值勤護士對伍德太太作自我介紹，並為她簡介病房。介紹的內容包括醫院的設備和病房、病床、以及必需品和貴重物品的保存方法。向入院病人作完簡介之後，照例會說聲「我待會兒再來」，走出病房。

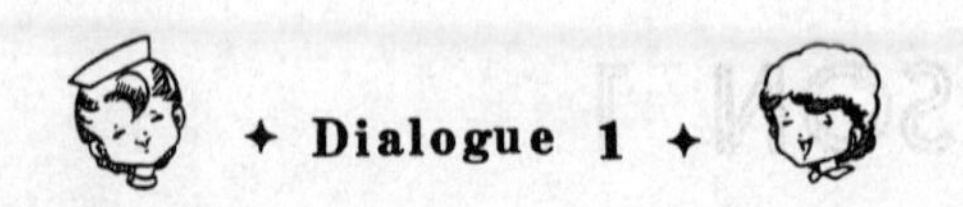

✦ Dialogue 1 ✦

Nurse: Hello.
Mrs. Wood: Hello.

Nurse: Are you Mrs. Wood?
Mrs. Wood: Yes.

Nurse: I am (Miss) Lin, your nurse today. How do you do?
Mrs. Wood: How do you do, Miss Lin?

Nurse: I will take you to your bed. ***Will you come this way***?

✦ Dialogue 2 ✦

Nurse: This is the bathroom. You may use it from 7 in the morning until 8 in the evening. Here on your right is a toilet. If this is occupied, there is another one over there.

✦ Dialogue 3 ✦

Nurse: Here is your bed. The call button is here. ***Please push the button this way when you want a nurse's help.*** When you are calling us, the light is on like that. Can you understand my explanation?
Mrs. Wood: Yes, I can. Thank you.

✦ 實況會話 1 ✦

護　士：嗨！

伍德太太：嗨！

護　士：您是伍德太太嗎？

伍德太太：是的。

護　士：我是林小姐，您今天的護士。您好。

伍德太太：您好，林小姐。

護　士：我帶您去您的床位，請跟我來好嗎？

✦ 實況會話 2 ✦

護　士：這是浴室，從早上七點到晚上八點可以使用。您的右邊是洗手間，如果這間有人使用，那邊還有一間。

✦ 實況會話 3 ✦

護　士：這是您的床位。呼叫鈕在這兒。當您需要護士幫助時，把鈕往這邊按。當您呼叫我們時，燈就像那樣亮著。您懂我的說明嗎？

伍德太太：是的，我懂，謝謝你。

✦ Dialogue 4 ✦

Nurse : This is your bedside table. Please keep only your small necessary items in it, such as toilet articles and changes. If you have any valuables, we will keep them for you in the hospital safe.

Mrs. Wood: Thank you.

✦ Dialogue 5 ✦

Nurse : Will you change into your nightgown or pajamas? Your doctor will come to visit you soon. I will come back in a few minutes.

**

nightgown〔'naɪt,gaʊn〕*n.*（長的）睡衣

●字彙備忘欄●

toilet article 盥洗用品
hospital safe 醫院的保險箱
denture, false teeth 假牙
apparatus〔,æpə'retəs〕*n.* 儀器
utility〔ju'tɪlətɪ〕*n.* 效用
pantry〔'pæntrɪ〕*n.* 餐具室
treatment room 治療室
registration office 掛號處
administration office 總務處

✦ 實況會話 4 ✦

護　士：這是您的床頭櫃。請您只放置盥洗用具，和零錢等小件必需用品。如果您有什麼貴重物品，我們幫您保管在醫院的保險箱裏。

伍德太太：謝謝你。

✦ 實況會話 5 ✦

護　士：您要換上睡衣嗎？醫生馬上會來看您。我待會兒再來。

** ─────────

pajamas〔pə'dʒæməz〕*n.* 睡衣

《護理重點》

1. 說話時可坐在椅子上，使眼睛的位置和對方在同一水平，且應注視對方的眼睛交談。
2. 詢問病患是否了解自己的說明。
3. 若院方有貴重物品保管、會客時間及衣物清洗等等規定時，應及早說明。
4. 有些病人會提出問題，以瞭解醫院的種種規定事項，無論如何，讓病人明瞭醫院狀況，可以減少許多痲煩和困擾。

護士必背英語句型

1. ***Will you come this way?***
   ♧ I will show your way.
   ♧ Please come along with me. 請跟我來。
2. ***When you want a nurse's help, please push the button.***
   ♧ When you need a nurse, please push this.
   ♧ When you desire assistance, please push this.
   當您需要護士幫忙時，請按這個鈕。
3. ***Please feel free to ask anything.***
   ♧ Please don't hesitate to ask.
   ♧ Please stop me when you have any questions.
   有什麼問題儘管問。
4. ***Please take your clothes off.***
   ♧ Please get undressed.
   ♧ Please remove your clothes. 請脫下衣服。
5. ***Please turn off the light.***
   ♧ Please switch off the light.
   ♧ Please turn the light off. 請關燈。
6. ***You can dress now.***
   ♧ Please get dressed now.
   ♧ Please get your clothes on. 請穿上衣服。

LESSON 2

飲食與檢查

Food Preference and Laboratory Examination

通常住院病患最關心的是伙食問題，所以護士向患者詢問他喜歡吃的食物。然後又將醫師的指示告訴患者，這指示包括要做許多檢查。

她馬上為病患抽血，並要病人將抽血部位，用棉花稍稍按一會兒。

✦ Dialogue 1 ✦

Nurse: ***What kind of food would you like to have, Western or Chinese***? The Chinese diet is included in your room charge. The Western diet is extra. ***You can also alternate the two styles*** if you would like to.

Mrs. Wood: Oh, that is very nice. But I don't have much of an appetite. So I would like something light and simple. I think I would like Chinese style for now.

✦ Dialogue 2 ✦

Nurse: Hello, Mrs. Wood. How are you feeling?

Mrs. Wood: ***I was tired*** but I'm feeling a little better now. I guess because I was so busy getting ready to come to the hospital.

Nurse: I am glad to hear you are feeling better. I just had a phone call from your doctor, Dr. Chen, and he has an emergency operation. So he asked me to tell you that he will see you this afternoon as early as possible.

Mrs. Wood: Oh, really?

** ———

room charge 病房費用

alternate 〔ˈɔltɚ͵net〕 *vt*. 交替

✦ 實況會話 1 ✦

護　士：您想吃什麼食物，中餐還是西餐？中餐包括在您的病房費用，西餐則是另外付費。如果您喜歡，也可以交替食用這兩種菜式。

伍德太太：噢，那很不錯，但是我沒有什麼食慾。所以，我想吃些清淡而簡單的。我現在想吃中餐。

✦ 實況會話 2 ✦

護　士：嗨，伍德太太，您覺得怎樣呢？

伍德太太：我很累，但現在覺得好些了，我想是因爲我太匆忙準備來醫院的關係。

護　士：很高興聽到你覺得好點了。我剛剛接到您的醫師——陳大夫的電話，他有一個緊急手術，所以他請我告訴您，他今天下午會儘早來看你。

伍德太太：哦，眞的嗎？

**

appetite〔'æpə,taɪt〕*n.* 食慾
emergency operation 緊急手術

✦ Dialogue 3 ✦

Nurse : ***He also said that this morning we should do some necessary tests*** and fill in this medical form.

Mrs. Wood : O.K. What kind of tests must I have?

Nurse : All the standard testings, like urine specimen, blood samples, ECG and X rays. ***Miss Wang who is a nurse's aid will take you to have those done.*** Then your nurse will help you fill out your medical form.

✦ Dialogue 4 ✦

Nurse : Now I'd like to take a blood sample. Will you put your arm here, and make a fist like this? You may feel a slight prick but it won't hurt much.

Mrs. Wood : That's good. I don't like to do this.

Nurse : Lots of people feel that way. Thank you. Did it hurt?

Mrs. Wood : No, not at all. You are really an expert. I hardly felt a thing.

Nurse : Oh, really? I'm so glad to hear that.

** ———

ECG 是 electrocardiogram 〔ɪ,lɛktro'kardɪə,græm〕 心電圖的縮寫

✦ 實況會話 3 ✦

護　士：他還說我們今天早上應該做些必要的檢驗，並填入這張醫療單中。

伍德太太：好的，我必須做哪些檢驗呢？

護　士：都是些普通的檢驗，例如驗尿、抽血、心電圖和X光等等。護士助理王小姐會帶你去做那些檢驗。然後，您的護士會爲您填醫療單。

✦ 實況會話 4 ✦

護　士：現在我要抽血了，請把手放在這兒，像這樣握拳好嗎？您可能會感到些微刺痛，但不會太痛。

伍德太太：那還好。我不喜歡抽血。

護　士：很多人也這麼覺得。謝謝，疼嗎？

伍德太太：不，一點都不疼。你眞的是專家，我幾乎沒什麼感覺。

護　士：哦，眞的嗎？很高興聽你這麼說。

---

a slight prick 些微的刺痛

expert 〔ˈɛkspɜt〕 *n.* 專家

✦ Dialogue 5 ✦

Nurse : I would like you to ***press down firmly*** like this for a few minutes.

Mrs. Wood : Is it all right now if I stop?

Nurse : Sure. That's enough.

● 字彙備忘欄 ●

solid diet 固體食物
liquid diet 流質食物
bland diet 無刺激性的食物
insurance [ɪn'ʃʊrəns] *n*. 保險
invoice ['ɪnvɔɪs] *n*. 發票
specimen ['spɛsəmən] *n*. 樣品；標本
be included 包含在內
be excluded 除了…以外
digestable [daɪ'dʒɛstəbl] *adj*. 可消化的
restriction on diet 飲食的限制

✦ 實況會話 5 ✦

護　士： 希望您像這樣緊壓幾分鐘。

伍德太太： 我現在可以停止了嗎？

護　士： 可以，夠了。

《護理重點》

1. 飲食方面
   a） 由於醫院伙食和餐館的伙食不同，必須問明外國病患，要吃中餐還是吃西餐。
   b） 有些外國人吃中餐時，以麵包代替米飯，以叉子代替筷子，因此也要附帶詢問。
2. 醫師晚來應診或檢查時，應簡單地向病患說明理由。

護士必背英語句型

1. ***What kind of food would you like to have, Western or Chinese?***
   ♧ Which do you prefer, Western or Chinese?
   ♧ Which do you want, Western or Chinese?
   您要吃什麼食物，西餐還是中餐？

2. ***You can also alternate the two styles.***
   ♧ Alternating the two styles is possible.
   ♧ You can eat either Chinese or Western by prior arrangement. 您也可以交替地吃這兩種菜式。

3. ***He said that we should do some necessary tests this morning.***
   ♧ He has ordered some necessary tests to be done this morning.
   ♧ He asked us to do some necessary tests this morning.
   他指示我們今早應該做些必要的檢驗。

4. ***Miss Wang who is a nurse's aid will take you to have those tests done.***
   ♧ Miss Wang who is a nurse's aid will take you to the lab to have those tests done.
   護士助理王小姐會帶您去做那些檢驗。

5. ***Please press down firmly on this spot.*** 請緊壓這個地方。
   ♧ Please press down here firmly. 請緊壓這裏。
   ♧ Please hold your arm tight like this.
   請像這樣緊握您的手臂。

LESSON 3

水分攝取量、排泄量的測定及特殊檢查

Measuring Liquid Intake and Output and Special Examination

護士必須測定24小時內，病患的水份攝取量和排泄量，並告訴病患一些應該注意的事情。

要做特殊檢查時，須事先告訴病人飲食方面應注意的事項、和造影劑的服用方法，並且說明服用後必然的反應，以使病人先有心理準備。

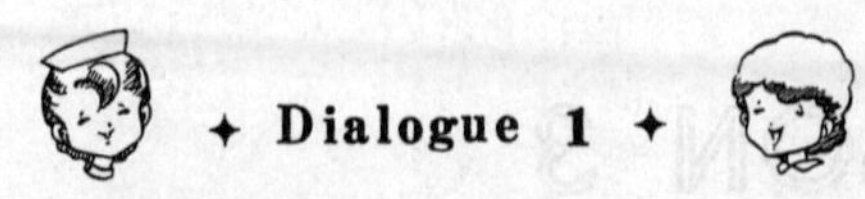

✦ Dialogue 1 ✦

Nurse : Your doctor has ordered us ***to measure all liquids that you take and eliminate***. This is done on a 24 hour basis from 6 in the morning until 6 in the following morning. All the fluid on your tray is measured but you may drink extra fluid if you wish on your own.

Mrs. Wood : You mean if I drink tea or juice in the coffee shop ?

Nurse : Yes, that's right. And about ***collecting urine***, ***please use the urine cup*** and ***place it into your urine collecting bag***, so that we can measure that too.

** ———————————

eliminate〔ɪ'lɪmə,net〕*v*. 排洩 fluid〔'fluɪd〕*n*. 流體

護 士： 您的主治大夫交代我們測量您所攝取與排泄的水份，這是以早晨六點到隔天早晨六點的二十四個小時爲單位進行的。我們已測量了您所吃食物裏的水份，您可以隨意喝您想喝的東西。

伍德太太： 你是指我可以到咖啡屋喝茶或果汁嗎？

護 士： 是的。至於採集尿液，請您用尿杯盛著放入您的尿袋，這樣，我們也可以測定那些。

**

urine〔'jurɪn〕*n.* 尿

✦ Dialogue 2 ✦

Nurse : You are scheduled to have a GI and a GB test tomorrow morning.

Mrs. Wood : Yes.

Nurse : Please have a regular supper at 5 o'clock. Then you will take one white tablet at 7 o'clock and wait and see if it has any kind of reaction on you. If not, you will take the rest of the three tablets.

Mrs. Wood : What do you mean by a reaction?

Nurse : Oh, nothing serious but perhaps a slight rash, loose bowels, or nauseous feeling.

Mrs. Wood : If that happens, should I tell you?

Nurse : Yes. Please don't eat or drink anything until the test is over. I'm sorry but ***you have to have an absolute empty stomach.***

** ———

GI = gastrointestinal [ˌgæstroɪn ˈtɛstɪnəl] *adj.* 胃腸的

✦實況會話 2✦

護　士：您預定於明天早上作胃腸檢查和膽囊檢查。

伍德太太：好的。

護　士：請在五點照常吃晚餐。然後在七點鐘服下一顆白色藥丸，等待看看有沒有什麼反應，如果沒有，在十一點時服用其他三顆藥。

伍德太太：你所謂的反應是指什麼？

護　士：哦，沒什麼大不了的，只是可能有輕微的發疹，拉肚子或嘔吐的感覺。

伍德太太：如果發生那些情況，要告訴你嗎？

護　士：是的。在檢查結束之前請不要吃喝任何東西。我很抱歉，您得完全空著胃。

**

nauseous〔'nɔʒəs〕*adj.* 作嘔的　　GB = gall bladder 膽囊

● 字彙備忘欄 ●

measure 〔 'mɛʒɚ 〕 *v*. 測量
intake 〔 'ɪn,tek 〕 *n*. 入口；攝取
elimination 〔 ɪ,lɪmə'neʃən 〕 *n*. 排泄
be scheduled 預定
gastro-intestinal examination 腸胃檢查
amination 〔 ,æmə'neʃən 〕 *n*. 氨化
reaction 〔 rɪ'ækʃən 〕 *n*. 反作用；反應
rash 〔 ræʃ 〕 *n*. 發疹
side effect 副作用
loose bowel 腹瀉
diarrhea 〔 ,daɪə'riə 〕 *n*. 腹瀉
bowel movement 排便
vomit 〔 'vɑmɪt 〕 *v*. 嘔吐
throw up 嘔吐
emesis 〔 'ɛməsɪs 〕 *n*. 〔醫〕嘔吐

《護理重點》

1. 應該清楚地說明檢查前的注意事項，特別是些緊急事項或時間事項，應記入備忘欄，親手交給患者。
2. 檢驗的反應，使用造影劑可能產生的副作用等，都應該先對病人說明如何應對。
3. 需要24小時內採尿的時候，要注意以下的用法：
   a）您可自行採取。
   b）以二十四小時爲準。
   c）從早晨六時起，到第二天早晨六時止。
4. 說明採集方法和處理方式的時候，應該詳示必需用品，並示範給病人看。
5. 同意書需由醫師寫下手術名稱，並於手術之前對病人加以解說，以徵求患者本身的同意簽署。

護士必背英語句型

1. We have to measure all liquids that you take in and eliminate.
   ♧ We need to know the amount of your ***liquids of intake and elimination.*** 我們必須了解您攝取及排泄的水份。

2. This test is done ***on a 24 hour basis*** from 6 in the morning until 6 in the following morning.
   ♧ You have to do this for 24 hours from 6 in the morning until 6 in the following morning.
   這個檢查是以早晨六點到第二天早上六點的二十四小時爲單位進行的。

3. ***You may drink extra fluid if you wish on your own.***
   ♧ You may drink ***freely.***
   ♧ You may have something to drink ***whenever you wish.***
   您可以隨意喝您想喝的東西。

4. ***To collect urine, please use a cup.***
   ♧ Use this cup to collect your urine.
   ♧ Please use this cup for collecting urine.
   請用這個杯子採集尿液。

5. ***Please place your urine in the bag.*** 請將尿倒入這個袋子。
   ♧ Please use this container for your urine.
   請將尿放進這個容器內。
   ♧ Please pour your urine into the bottle.
   請把尿倒入這個瓶子之中。

6. ***You have to have an absolute empty stomach.***
   ♧ Your stomach must be empty. 您得完全空著胃。

LESSON 4

治療・給藥

Treatment and Medication

護士為了給伍德太太進行輕微、有效的灌腸，向她說明躺臥的方法。

給藥時，必須向病患簡單地介紹口服藥的效果及作用。然後打針，同樣地也必須向病人解釋針劑有安眠的副作用。

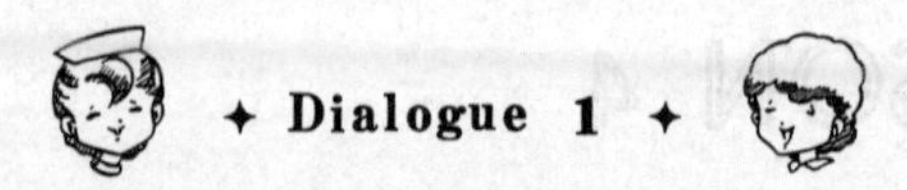

✦ Dialogue 1 ✦

Nurse : ***You seem to be constipated***. I'd like to give you a glycerine enema right now.

Mrs. Wood : O.K. Which side should I lie down on?

Nurse : On your left side, please. Now open your mouth and breathe slowly. That's right. ***You may feel like you have to have a bowel movement*** but hold it until you can't stand it any longer. ***When you are finished, don't flush it***. I need to see your bowel movements.

**

glycerine〔'glɪsərɪn〕*n.* 甘油

✦ Dialogue 2 ✦

Nurse : Here is your medicine, Mrs. Wood.

Mrs. Wood : What's this for?

Nurse : It's medicine for your heart.

Mrs. Wood : Oh, am I having trouble with my heart?

Nurse : It's nothing to worry about. This just aids your heart beat.

✦ 實況會話 1 ✦

護　士：您似乎便祕了，我想立刻給您甘油灌腸。

伍德太太：好的。我該躺那一邊？

護　士：請躺左邊。現在張開嘴巴並慢慢地呼吸，就是這樣。您會覺得想上大號，但是請您忍耐到您無法忍耐時才去。排便後請不要沖掉，我必須檢查您的糞便。

** ──────────

bowel movements 通便；糞便

✦ 實況會話 2 ✦

護　士：伍德太太，這是您的藥。

伍德太太：幹什麼用的？

護　士：這是您的心臟藥。

伍德太太：哦，我的心臟有問題嗎？

護　士：沒什麼好擔心的，只是增進您的心跳罷了。

✦ Dialogue 3 ✦

Nurse : I have an injection for you. I would like to give this injection on your buttocks.

Mrs. Wood : O.K.

Nurse : This medicine may make you feel sleepy, but don't worry. It's just a reaction of the medicine. So ***please stay in bed following this injection.***

** ─────────

injection〔ɪn'dʒɛkʃən〕*n.* 注射

• 字彙備忘欄 •

constipation〔ˌkɑnstəˈpeʃən〕*n.* [醫] 便祕
enema〔ˈɛnəmə〕*n.* [醫] 灌腸
cramp〔kræmp〕*n.* 抽筋
laxative〔ˈlæksətɪv〕*adj.* 通便的 *n.* 通便劑
flush〔flʌʃ〕*v.* 沖洗
medication〔ˌmɛdɪˈkeʃən〕*n.* 藥物治療
effect〔əˈfɛkt〕*n.* 效力
side effect 副作用
good result 結果良好
buttocks〔ˈbʌtəks〕*n.* 臀

✦實況會話 3✦

護　士：我幫您打針，打在臀部。

伍德太太：好的。

護　士：這藥會使您想睡覺，但是不要擔心，那只是一種藥物反應而已。所以打下這針之後請躺在床上。

《護理重點》

1. 灌腸之前，必須先告訴病患廁所的位置。進行的時候，應該和病人說說話，以緩和他緊張的情緒。由於要檢查結果和性質，排泄物均不可沖掉，這點非常重要，須說明清楚。
2. 一定要完全了解吃藥的時刻、藥品名稱與服用的效果或作用，病人問起時才能有所交代，尤其是藥品的作用，一定要和醫生先研究清楚後，再加以說明。

　　若有患者開車前來診治，其病況不宜駕車時，需特別提醒其注意。

護士必背英語句型

1. ***You seem to be constipated.***
   - ♧ You seem to be having constipation.
   - ♧ You seem to have constipation.　您似乎有便祕。

2. ***Which side*** should I lie down on?
   - ♧ ***How*** shall I lie down?
   - ♧ ***Which way*** should I lie down?　我該躺哪一側呢？

3. You may ***feel as if*** you have to ***have a bowel movement.***
   - ♧ You may feel as if you have to ***go to the toilet.***
   - ♧ Maybe, you will ***feel like*** going to the toilet right away.
     您可能會感覺想上廁所。

4. ***You can't stand it any longer.***
   - ♧ You are not able to ***bear it*** any longer.
   - ♧ It is hard for you to ***take it*** any longer.
     您不能再忍耐下去。

5. When you are finished, don't flush it.
   - ♧ Please leave it in the toilet after you are finished.
     排便後（不要把它沖掉。）請把它留在那兒。

6. Please ***stay in bed*** following this medicine.
   - ♧ Please ***lie in bed*** after this medicine.
   - ♧ Please ***rest in bed*** after this medicine.
     吃完這個藥請在床上休息。

LESSON 5

從患者處收集資料

Information Gathering

護士小姐走到今天剛入院的金太太病房去，詢問她的日常生活、家庭背景、職業、雙親、對食物的偏好、一天的運動量等個人資料，並確定是否因宗教信仰，而有食物方面的限制。

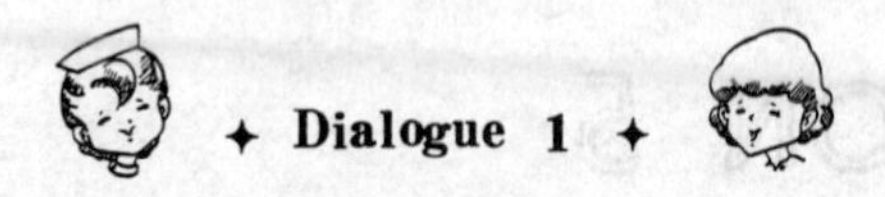

✦ Dialogue 1 ✦

Nurse : ***I would like to ask you some questions for our records***, Mrs. King.

Mrs. King : What about? What kind of questions?

Nurse : Well, personal things such as your eating habits and some of your clinical history.

Mrs. King : All right.

Nurse : ***What do you do for a living***?

Mrs. King : I am a clerk working in a company.

**

clinical history 病歷

✦ Dialogue 2 ✦

Nurse : Do you live with your family?

Mrs. King : No, I live by myself.

Nurse : Are your parents living?

Mrs. King : No, they died several years ago.

Nurse : ***What was the cause of the death***?

Mrs. King : My father died of a heart attack in 1975, and my mother died of old age.

✦實況會話 1✦

護　士：金太太，我想請問您幾個要記錄的問題。

金太太：關於什麼的？是些什麼問題呢？
護　士：唔…，您個人的問題，像您的飲食習慣、病歷等等。

金太太：好的。
護　士：您從事什麼工作？
金太太：我是一家公司的辦事員。

✦實況會話 2✦

護　士：您和家人住在一塊兒嗎？
金太太：不，我自己住。
護　士：您的父母健在嗎？
金太太：不，他們幾年前去世了。
護　士：死因是什麼？
金太太：我父親1975年因心臟病發作死亡，我母親是因年老而死的。

✦ Dialogue 3 ✦

Nurse : ***Do you have a good appetite?***

Mrs. King : Yes, I have.

Nurse : What kind of food do you dislike? Please tell me if there is something in particular that you do not like or can not eat.

Mrs. King : Oh, I eat everything but I prefer fish rather than meat.

Nurse : What is your religion? Is there any food you don't eat for religious reasons?

Mrs. King : Yes, I don't eat meat on Fridays.

Nurse : All right, I will inform the dietitian about this. Thank you, Mrs. King.

** ———————————

dietitian 〔,daɪə'tɪʃən〕 *n.* 營養師

✦ Dialogue 4 ✦

Nurse : I would like to ask a few questions about your daily life.

Mrs. King : All right.

Nurse : What time do you usually get up?

Mrs. King : At 6 o'clock and then I go for a walk.

Nurse : Oh, how far do you walk? Do you go jogging, too?

Mrs. King : Yes. ***I think it's a very good way to stay healthy.***

✦ 實況會話 3 ✦

護　士：您的胃口好嗎？
金太太：很好。
護　士：您不喜歡哪種食物？如果您有什麼特別不喜歡吃或不能吃的東西，請告訴我。

金太太：噢，我什麼都吃，但我比較喜歡魚而不喜歡肉。

護　士：您信什麼教？有什麼宗教理由而不吃的食物嗎？

金太太：有的，我星期五不吃肉。
護　士：好的，我會轉達給醫院裏的營養師。謝謝您，金太太。

✦ 實況會話 4 ✦

護　士：我想問有關您日常生活的幾個問題。

金太太：好的。
護　士：您通常幾點起床。
金太太：六點起床然後去散步。
護　士：噢，走多遠呢？您也慢跑嗎？
金太太：是的，我認爲那是保持健康的好方法。

Nurse : Good for you. I think so, too. Do you do any sports?

Mrs. King : No, not really.

Nurse : Do you take the bus when you go to work or do you go by car?

Mrs. King : I take the bus.

Nurse : Do you work sitting at a desk for the whole day?

Mrs. King : Yes, and really feel the need to get up and exercise.

Nurse : Do you feel a shortness of breath when you go up the stairways?

Mrs. King : Yes, a little, but ***it does not bother me***.

Nurse : That is a good sign. Thank you, Mrs. King.

** ————————

Good for you. 好！不錯！

●字彙備忘欄●

record〔'rɛkɚd〕*n.* 記錄
eating habit 飲食習慣
for a living 謀生
heart attack 心臟病發作
religion〔rɪ'lɪdʒən〕*n.* 宗教
shortness of breath 喘不過氣
under the care of a doctor 在醫生照料下

護　士：好，我也這麼認爲。您做運動嗎？

金太太：不，我沒有。

護　士：您搭公車上班還是開車上班？

金太太：我搭公車。

護　士：您從事整天坐著的工作嗎？

金太太：是的，所以我眞正覺得有必要起來運動。

護　士：爬樓梯的時候，您會覺得喘不過氣來嗎？

金太太：是的，有一點，但對我並沒有妨礙。

護　士：那是個好現象。謝謝您，金太太。

●字彙備忘欄●

chief complaint 主訴

suspect〔sə'spɛkt〕*v.* 猜想

outpatient department 門診部

sibling〔'sɪblɪŋ〕*n.* 兄弟姊妹

observation〔ˌɑbzɚ'veʃən〕*n.* 觀察

護士必背英語句型

1. ***What do you do for a living?***
   - ♧ What is your job?
   - ♧ What is your occupation? 您從事什麼工作?

2. ***Do you have a good appetite?***
   - ♧ How is your appetite coming along?
   - ♧ Do you feel like eating? 您的胃口好嗎?

3. ***I think it's a very good way to stay healthy.***
   - ♧ I believe it's a good way to keep my health.
   - ♧ I suppose it's very good for the health.

     我認爲那是保持健康的好方法。

4. ***It does not bother me.***
   - ♧ It is O. K. with me.
   - ♧ It is all right with me. 那對我並沒有妨礙。

LESSON 6

觀察病痛・詢問是否有藥物過敏

Observing the Patient in Pain and Asking about Allergy

護士小姐觀察金太太的病痛，並詢問她病痛的種類、持續的時間、及何時開始疼痛等資料。

然後確定她對藥物有沒有過敏現象，以及現在是否服用任何藥物。

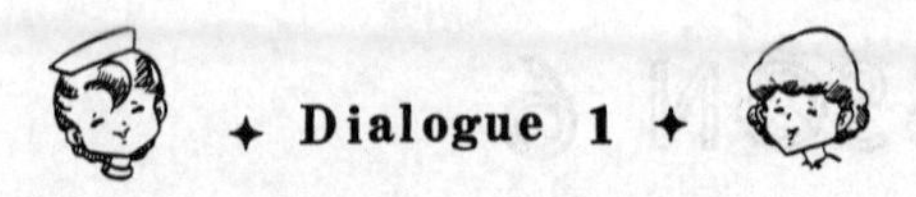

✦ Dialogue 1 ✦

Nurse: What is the matter?

Mrs. King: I have pain.

Nurse: Where is the pain? Please show me where it is.

Mrs. King: Right here on this side of my stomach.

Nurse: ***What kind of a pain is it***, a burning pain, or a dull pain?

**

burning〔'bɝnɪŋ〕*adj.* 激烈的　　burning pain 灼痛

✦ Dialogue 2 ✦

Nurse: ***How long have you had this pain***?

Mrs. King: Since yesterday afternoon.

Nurse: How long does the pain last? Do you feel the pain constantly or every ***once in a while***?

Mrs. King: Every once in a while it comes suddenly.

Nurse: ***Is it very hard to bear***?

Mrs. King: Yes, I can hardly bear the pain.

✦ 實況會話 1 ✦

護　士： 怎麼回事？

金太太： 我感到疼痛。

護　士： 哪兒痛？請指給我看。

金太太： 胃的這一邊，就是這裏。

護　士： 怎麼痛法，是灼痛還是鈍痛？

** ――――――――――――

dull〔dʌll〕*adj.* 隱約的　　　dull pain 鈍痛

✦ 實況會話 2 ✦

護　士： 痛多久了？

金太太： 從昨天下午開始。

護　士： 疼痛持續多久？是持續性的疼痛，還是陣痛？

金太太： 是突發的陣痛。

護　士： 痛得難以忍受嗎？

金太太： 是的，我幾乎無法忍受這種疼痛。

✦ Dialogue 3 ✦

Nurse: ***Are you allergic to anything?***

Mrs. King: What do you mean?

Nurse: Let me see, do you break out in a rash when you eat certain food?

Mrs. King: No, I don't.

Nurse: Do you have a reaction to any medicine?

Mrs. King: Yes, when I take aspirin, I get a rash all over my body.

**

rash〔ræʃ〕*n.* 發疹

✦ Dialogue 4 ✦

Nurse: ***Have you been hospitalized before?*** Have you had any diseases before?

Mrs. King: No.

Nurse: ***Are you on any medication?*** If you are, I would like to know the name of the medicine.

Mrs. King: No. I'm not taking any medicine, but I do take vitamins every day.

Nurse: Do you have (any) difficulty sleeping? How many hours do you usually sleep at night?

✦ 實 況 會 話 3 ✦

護　士：您對什麼東西過敏嗎？

金太太：什麼意思？

護　士：我想想看，您吃某種食物時，會突然發疹嗎？

金太太：不會。

護　士：您對任何葯物過敏嗎？

金太太：是的，我吃阿司匹靈時會全身發疹。

✦ 實 況 會 話 4 ✦

護　士：您以前曾經住過院嗎？曾經生過病嗎？

金太太：沒有。

護　士：您目前有沒有服用任何葯物？如果有，我想知道葯物的名稱。

金太太：不，我現在沒有服用任何葯物，但我每天都吃維他命。

護　士：您會失眠嗎？通常晚上睡幾小時？

Mrs. King : About 5 to 6 hours.

Nurse : Do you wake up during the night ?

Mrs. King : Yes.

Nurse : How many times ? Once or more ?

Mrs. King : At least twice.

Nurse : Because you have to go to the toilet ? Thank you for your cooperation, Mrs. King.

** ——

medication〔ˌmɛdɪˈkeʃən〕*n.* 葯物（治療）

●字彙備忘欄●

stomach〔ˈstʌmək〕*n.* 胃
bear〔bɛr〕*v.* 忍受
allergy〔ˈæləˑdʒɪ〕*n.* 過敏症
allergic reaction 過敏反應
constantly〔ˈkɑnstəntlɪ〕*adv.* 持續地
feel uncomfortable 覺得不舒服
bleeding〔ˈblidɪŋ〕*n.* 出血
the right-hand side of abdomen 右側腹部
various causes 各種原因
overwork〔ˈovəˈwɝk〕*n.* 操勞過度
avoid〔əˈvɔɪd〕*v.* 避免

金太太： 大約五至六個鐘頭。

護 士： 您半夜會醒過來嗎？

金太太： 會。

護 士： 幾次？一次或更多次？

金太太： 至少兩次。

護 士： 因爲您得上厠所對不對？謝謝您的合作，金太太。

** ——————————

vitamin〔'vaɪtəmɪn〕*n.* 維他命

《護理重點》

1. 如必須確定疼痛部位，及觀察皮膚變化時，務請病人脫掉衣服，並試觸其疼痛部位。
2. 必須十分具體地詢問藥物過敏的狀況，順便要詢問其何以服用現在服用的藥物。

護士必背英語句型

1. ***What kind of a pain is it?***
   - ♧ What is the pain like?
   - ♧ What type of pain is it? 怎麼痛法？

2. ***How long have you had this pain?*** 痛多久了？
   - ♧ Since when have you had this pain?
   - ♧ When did this pain start? 什麼時候開始痛的？

3. ***Once in a while?***
   - ♧ Now and then?
   - ♧ Sometimes? 陣痛嗎？

4. ***Is it very hard to bear?***
   - ♧ Is the pain unbearable?
   - ♧ Can't you stand this pain? 痛得難以忍受嗎？

5. ***Are you allergic to anything?***
   - ♧ Do you have an allergic reaction to anything?
   - ♧ Have you ever had an allergic reaction to anything?
     您對什麼東西過敏嗎？

6. ***Have you been hospitalized before?***
   - ♧ Have you been admitted to a hospital before?
   - ♧ Have you ever been hospitalized? 以前曾經住過院嗎？

7. ***Are you on any medication?***
   - ♧ Are you taking medicine at this present time?
   - ♧ Are you taking any medicine now?
     您目前服用任何藥物嗎？

LESSON 7

對糖尿病患者的指示

Instruction for a Diabetic Patient

在進行糖尿病患者的飲食治療之前，應先詢問患者的飲食習慣。具體地說明對酒的種類、份量及卡路里的限制。並讓患者明瞭飲食治療法的效果，以增進患者的信心。

✦ Dialogue 1 ✦

Nurse : I need to ask you some questions about your eating habits.

Mrs. King : Yes, but why?

Nurse : As the doctor has explained to you, it's necessary to have a new diet.

Mrs. King : Yes, because I am a diabetic.

Nurse : All right. First of all, I need to know your eating habits before we talk about your new diet.

Mrs. King : O. K. Please feel free to ask anything you wish.

Nurse : ***Do you eat out often***?

Mrs. King : Maybe three times a month.

Nurse : Do you drink at all?

Mrs. King : Yes, I do.

Nurse : What do you drink?

Mrs. King : Wine. I usually drink it with dinner and before I go to bed.

Nurse : How much do you drink at one time?

Mrs. King : Usually a glass of wine with dinner and a small bottle before I go to bed.

Nurse : That makes a total of a quart a day. Thank you, Mrs. King.

** ───────────────

diabetic 〔,daɪə'bɛtɪk〕 *n.* 糖尿病患者

護　士：我必須請問您一些有關飲食習慣的問題。

金太太：好的，不過做什麼呢？

護　士：正如醫師向您解釋過的，必須進行新的飲食治療法。

金太太：是的，因爲我是糖尿病患者。

護　士：好的。首先，在談新的飲食治療法之前，我必須了解您的飲食習慣。

金太太：好的。請儘管問你想問的吧。

護　士：您常在外面吃飯嗎？

金太太：大概一個月三次。

護　士：您喝不喝酒呢？

金太太：是的，我喝。

護　士：您喝什麼呢？

金太太：葡萄酒。我通常在晚餐及睡前喝。

護　士：您一次喝多少？

金太太：通常晚餐喝一杯葡萄酒，睡前喝一小瓶。

護　士：那樣一天總共喝一夸特。謝謝您，金太太。

**

quart〔kwɔrt〕*n.* 夸脫（等於四分之一加侖）

✦ Dialogue 2 ✦

Nurse: The doctor has ordered a two-thousand-calorie daily diet for you, and it might make you a little hungry at first, but you will get used to it.

Mrs. King: O. K. I will try.

Nurse: As part of trying to lower calorie count, it will be best to ***reduce your intake*** of wine since wine has a lot of calories.

Mrs. King: May I see the pamphlet, please?

Nurse: See, there are 80 calories in 100 cc of wine, and no calories in 70cc of whisky or brandy, 70cc of whisky equals two glasses of whisky with ice and water, and 35cc of brandy equals a regular-sized brandy glass.

** ———

calorie〔ˈkælərɪ〕*n.* 卡路里

✦ Dialogue 3 ✦

Nurse: How are you this morning?

Mrs. King: I am very hungry.

Nurse: I know how you feel. ***You are doing very well.*** So your condition will soon be better.

Mrs. King: Do you think so?

Nurse: Yes, your urine test for sugar was two plus this morning which is ***a lot better than before.***

✦ 實況會話 2 ✦

護　士： 醫師指示您每天吃兩千卡路里的飲食，起先您可能會覺得有點餓，但您會習慣的。

金太太： 好的，我試試看。

護　士： 爲了試著減低卡路里量，您最好減少葡萄酒的攝取量，因爲葡萄酒的卡路里很高。

金太太： 請讓我看看手册好嗎？

護　士： 看，100cc 的葡萄酒含有 80 卡路里，而 70cc 的威士忌或白蘭地，則沒有卡路里。70cc 的威士忌相當於兩杯摻冰和水的威士忌，而 35cc 的白蘭地等於普通白蘭地酒杯一杯的份量。

** ―――――――――――

intake〔'ɪn,tek〕*n.* 引入之物；攝取量

✦ 實況會話 3 ✦

護　士： 今天早上覺得如何？

金太太： 我好餓。

護　士： 我了解您的感受。您做得非常好，所以您的情況會很快好轉的。

金太太： 你這麼認爲嗎？

護　士： 是的，您今天早上做的尿糖檢驗是 2^+，比以前好多了。

Mrs. King : Oh, Yes?

Nurse : I am going to make an appointment for you with the dietician, so you can learn more about your diet.

** ————————————

urine〔'jʊrɪnə〕*n.* 尿

● 字彙備忘欄 ●

diet〔'daɪət〕*n.* 規定飲食
eat out 在外面吃飯
whisky with ice and water 加冰和水的威士忌
shot〔ʃɑt〕*v.* 試圖
get used to～習慣於～
reduce〔rɪ'djus〕*v.* 減少
appointment〔ə'pɔɪntmənt〕*n.* 約會
hyperglycemia〔,haɪpɚglaɪ'simɪə〕*n.*〔醫〕血糖過多症
hypoglycemia〔,haɪpoglaɪ'simɪə〕*n.*〔醫〕血糖過低症
increase〔ɪn'kris〕*v.* 血糖增加
blood pressure 血壓
order〔'ɔrdɚ〕*n.* 指示
urine sugar / blood sugar 尿糖／血糖

金太太：　哦，是嗎？

護　士：　我會替您和營養師約好，那樣您就能知道更多關於飲食療法的事。

護士必背英語句型

1. ***Do you eat out often?***
   - ♧ Do you go out for dinner frequently?
   - ♧ Do you eat out a lot?

   您常在外面吃飯嗎？

2. ***to reduce your intake***
   - ♧ to cut down on your intake
   - ♧ to bring down the amount of your intake

   減少攝取量

3. ***You are doing very well.*** 您做得非常好。
   - ♧ You are trying very hard. 您在努力地嘗試。
   - ♧ You are doing your best. 您儘力而爲了。

4. ***A lot better than before.***
   - ♧ Much better than before.
   - ♧ Making good improvement.

   比以前好多了。

LESSON 8

照顧限制塩分攝取的病患及和醫師連繫

Care for the Patient with Salt Free Diet and Connection with a Doctor

向進行限塩飲食治療法的金太太，詢問其食慾狀況，並以檢驗證明已有進展加以鼓勵。

接受金太太的請求和醫師連繫，並解釋聯繫的方式及結果。

✦ Dialogue 1 ✦

Nurse : Good afternoon, Mrs. King. ***Have you been resting*** and how are you feeling?

Mrs. King : I have been resting very well, but I still feel very weak.

Nurse : Are you using the urinary cup ***to measure your urine***?

Mrs. King : Yes.

Nurse : Very good. How is your appetite coming along?

Mrs. King : Things are still tasteless to me.

Nurse : Yes, food really tastes different without salt, but the lab test shows improvement. You need to be on salt-free diet.

Mrs. King : Oh, is that so?

✦ Dialogue 2 ✦

Nurse : Mrs. King, you said ***you wanted to see Dr. Ing*** today, didn't you?

Mrs. King : Yes, but I haven't seen him yet.

Nurse : All right, I will call and find out when he will come. Would you please wait a little while? I will come back soon and let you know.

Mrs. King : Oh, thank you. I'd appreciate that.

Nurse : Mrs. King, he is still in the outpatient department seeing many patients. He said he will come to see you by 2 o'clock. Will that be all right

✦ 實況會話 1 ✦

護　士：午安，金太太。您休息過了嗎？覺得怎麼樣？

金太太：已經充分休息過了，不過還是覺得很虛弱。

護　士：您用尿杯量過尿嗎？

金太太：量了。

護　士：很好。您胃口好不好呢？

金太太：吃東西還是感覺不出味道。

護　士：是的，無鹽食物嚐起來的確不太一樣，但是檢驗顯示已有改善。您得採取禁鹽飲食療法。

金太太：噢，是這樣嗎？

✦ 實況會話 2 ✦

護　士：金太太，您說今天想見應醫師，不是嗎？

金太太：是的，但是還沒見到他。

護　士：好的，我打電話問問看他什麼時候來。請您稍等一會兒好嗎？我馬上回來告訴您。

金太太：噢，謝謝。我很感激你那樣做。

護　士：金太太，他還在門診部有很多病人要看，他說兩點以前會來看您。這樣好嗎？

for you?

Mrs. King : Yes, fine, thank you.

** ———————————

outpatient department 門診部

✦ Dialogue 3 ✦

Nurse : ***I've kept ringing*** his office but ***I could not get in touch with him.***

Mrs. King : What shall I do then?

Nurse : I can leave your message on his desk if you want me to.

Mrs. King : Yes, please do that for me.

Nurse : I will call again tomorrow morning as soon as I come to work.

金太太： 好的，謝謝你。

✦ 實況會話 3 ✦

護　士： 我一直打到他的辦公室，但是找不到他。

金太太： 那麼我該怎麼辦呢？
護　士： 假如您要的話，我可以在他的桌上，替您留言。

金太太： 好的，麻煩你幫我留言。
護　士： 明天早上我一上班，就再打電話給他。

●字彙備忘欄●

feel weak 覺得虛弱
salt free 禁鹽
lab test (laboratory test) 檢驗
measure〔'mɛʒɚ〕*v.* 測量
urinary cup 尿杯
seeing patient 診療中
tasteless〔'testlɪs〕*adj.* 沒有味道的
nephritis〔nɛ'fraɪtɪs〕*n.*〔醫〕腎臟炎
acute nephritis 急性腎臟炎
hypertension〔'haɪpɚ'tɛnʃən〕*n.*〔醫〕高血壓
intake/output 攝取/排出
edema〔ɪ'dimɑ〕*n.*〔醫〕水腫;浮腫
pitting edema 凹陷浮腫
heart burn 心口灼熱
proteinuria〔'protiɪˌnjʊrɪə〕*n.*〔醫〕蛋白尿

《護理重點》

1. 限制鹽分攝取量，對患者來說是非常困擾的一件事，所以應該儘量鼓勵他們。
2. 要指導病人完全能夠自行採尿，及使用試紙檢驗，並要確認其行使之正確與否。
3. 如果病人請你和其主治醫師聯絡，應盡力執行並把結果告訴病人。
4. 如果要觀察病人身上浮腫等狀況時，應先知會病人「請讓我看看……」之後才開始檢視，絕不能悶聲不響地隨意進行。

護士必背英語句型

1. ***Have you been resting?***

   ♧ Are you in bed most of the time?

   ♧ Have you been keeping off your feet? 您休息過了嗎？

2. ***to measure your urine***

   ♧ to check the amount of urine

   ♧ to estimate the amount of urine 測量尿量

3. ***You need to be on a salt-free diet.***

   ♧ Your diet must be salt-free.

   ♧ You may not use any salt for cooking.
   您得採取禁鹽飲食療法。

4. ***You want to see Dr. Ing.***

   ♧ You want to talk with Dr. Ing.

   ♧ You want to make an appointment with Dr. Ing.
   您想見應大夫。

5. ***I've kept ringing.***

   ♧ I've kept calling.

   ♧ I've been trying to reach him. 我一直打電話。

6. ***I could not get in touch with him.***

   ♧ I couldn't find him.

   ♧ I couldn't reach him. 我找不到他。

LESSON 9

手術前的程序

Surgical Procedure

手術前，護士必須向病患告知接受手術的日期、手術預定的時刻、並確認手術的名稱。此外要向病人簡單說明手術前的準備工作、手術時由於麻醉作用而不會感到疼痛、如何避免手術後的併發症、以及麻醉藥效消失後可服用止痛劑等等。

✦ Dialogue 1 ✦

Nurse : I am sure that you know ***you are scheduled to have an operation*** tomorrow.

Mrs. Wood : Yes. But what time am I going to surgery?

Nurse : The operation starts at 9 o'clock. But you will get injections about 30 to 45 minutes before you leave for surgery. If your family comes to see you before the operation, they should come by 7:30 before you get injections. Otherwise, you may be falling asleep when they arrive at your bedside.

Mrs. Wood : Oh, I see.

Nurse : Did your doctor explain to you about what operation you are going to have?

Mrs. Wood : Yes. ***I am going to have surgery of removing my gall bladder.***

Nurse : All right. Have you signed the consent?

Mrs. Wood : Yes. Here it is.

** ———

gall bladder 膽囊

護　士： 相信您一定知道，您預定明天動手術。

伍德太太： 是的，但我什麼時候進手術室呢？

護　士： 手術九點開始。但在進手術室之前三十至四十五分鐘左右，得先打針。如果您的家人手術前要來看您應該在七點半，打針以前來。否則，當他們到達床邊時，您可能睡著了。

伍德太太： 噢，我知道了。

護　士： 您的醫師向您解釋過要動什麼手術了嗎？

伍德太太： 是的。我要動切除膽囊的手術。

護　士： 是的。同意書簽了嗎？

伍德太太： 簽了，在這裡。

✦ Dialogue 2 ✦

Nurse : I would like to explain the preparation for the operation. If you have any questions, please stop me.

Mrs. Wood : Yes.

Nurse : ***First of all, we will prepare you by shaving*** and cleansing. In your case, we will be shaving a wide area from under the breast to the lower abdomen. After shaving, we would like you to take a tub bath or shower.

Mrs. Wood : I see.

Nurse : You are going to have a liquid supper and you will get sleeping pills at 9. Absolutely nothing by mouth after midnight. In the early morning you will have an enema.

Mrs. Wood : Can I take a shower after the enema?

Nurse : Well, you are going to be very busy changing into a "patient gown", getting intravenous drip injection and injections for surgery. And soon you will be taken to the operating room. ***More than likely you will not have time.***

** ———

intravenous 〔,ɪntrə'vinəs〕 *adj.* 靜脈注射的

breast 〔brɛst〕 *n.* 胸部

✦實況會話 2 ✦

護　士：我要解釋手術的準備工作。如果您有任何疑問，請叫我停下來。

伍德太太：好的。

護　士：首先，我們要幫您剃毛及消毒，做手術前的準備工作。以您來說，要剃掉從胸部以下到下腹之間的一大部分。剃毛後，希望您洗個盆浴或淋浴。

伍德太太：知道了。

護　士：您要吃流質的晚餐，九點時服用安眠藥。午夜之後，絕對不許進食。一大早您就得灌腸。

伍德太太：灌腸後，我可以淋浴嗎？

護　士：唔，您要忙著更換「手術衣」，打靜脈內點滴注射及手術用的注射劑。而且不久就要送入開刀房，很可能不會有時間。

** ——————————

abdomen〔æb'domən〕*n.* 腹部

enema〔'ɛnəmɑ〕*n.* 灌腸

✦ Dialogue 3 ✦

Mrs. Wood : How long am I going to be in the operating room? I mean when will I be back to this room?

Nurse : It is hard to tell. It will depend on operation procedures and your recovery from the anesthesia. You will probably return to this room before the afternoon.

Mrs. Wood : I see.

Nurse : Mrs. Wood, you look worried. Do you have any problems?

Mrs. Wood : Nurse, will this operation hurt very much?

Nurse : Mrs. Wood, you are going to have general anesthesia. So during the operation you will not feel a thing. You will find yourself back in your room after the operation. You may feel some pain in a drowsy feeling. However if you can not stand the pain, please let us know, as your doctor has prescribed medicine to relieve the pain.

Mrs. Wood : Thanks. I feel a little bit relieved.

Nurse : An anesthesiologist will visit you soon.

** ——————————

anesthesia〔ˌænəsˈθiʒə〕*n.* 麻醉

✦ 實況會話 3 ✦

伍德太太：　我要在開刀房裡待多久呢？我是說什麼時候回到這間房間呢？

護　士：　很難說，得看手術的過程以及您從麻醉中復原的情形。很可能在下午以前回到病房。

伍德太太：　我知道了。

護　士：　伍德太太，您看起來好像很擔心。有什麼問題嗎？

伍德太太：　護士小姐，這種手術會很痛嗎？

護　士：　伍德太太，您將要全身麻醉，所以手術時會毫無知覺。手術後，您會發現自己回到病房了，也許覺得昏昏沈沈的有點痛。不過，如果痛得受不了，請告訴我們。因爲醫生開了止痛劑。

伍德太太：　謝謝，我稍微安心了。

護　士：　麻醉師馬上會來看您。

** ─────────────

anesthesiologist 〔,ænəs,θizɪ'ɑlədʒɪst〕 *n.* 麻醉師

●字彙備忘欄●

consent form 同意書
removal〔rɪ'muvl̩〕*n*. 切除
anesthesia〔ˌænəs'θiʒə〕*n*.〔醫〕痲醉
drowsy〔'draʊzɪ〕*adj*. 昏昏欲睡的
prescribe〔prɪ'skraɪb〕*v*. 開藥方
recover〔rɪ'kʌvɚ〕*v*. 痊癒；復元
be relieved 安心
minor〔'maɪnɚ〕*adj*. 較小的；未成年的
cholecystectomy〔ˌkɑləsɪs'tɛktəmɪ〕*n*.〔外科〕膽囊切除術

護士必背英語句型

1. ***You are scheduled to have an operation.***
   - ♧ You are going to have an operation.
   - ♧ You are posted to have an operation. 您預定要動手術。

2. ***I am going to have surgery for removal of my gall bladder.***
   - ♧ I am going to have a cholecystectomy.
   - ♧ I will undergo gall bladder surgery.

     我要動切除膽囊的手術。

3. ***First of all, we will prepare you by shaving.***
   - ♧ First, we will prep you by shaving the area where you will have your operation.
   - ♧ Now, we will prep you by shaving for your operation.

     首先，我們要幫您剃毛，做手術前的準備工作。

4. ***More than likely you will not have time.***
   - ♧ Probably you will not have time.
   - ♧ I am afraid you may not be able to have time.

     很可能不會有時間。

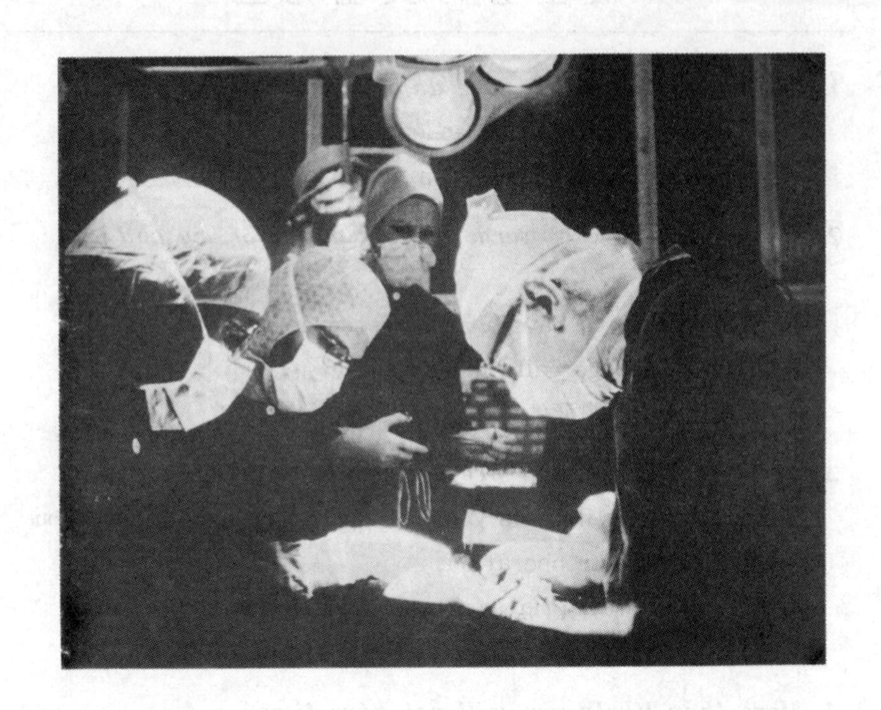

LESSON 10

手術當天的護理

Preoperation Care

手術當天，護士請伍德太太利用便盆，躺在床上排尿。

護士向病人說明必須插入鼻胃管的原因，並得到病人的合作，將鼻胃管吞下。然後要病人注意，雖然鼻胃管插入之後，有稍許不舒服的感覺，但千萬不要拔掉它，否則會產生非常大的麻煩。

✦ Dialogue 1 ✦

Nurse : ***Urinating after operations sometimes seems to be very hard***, because of the lying position and pulling feeling at the suture-site. Try urinating lying in bed just for exercise. I will leave a bed pan here. Just let us know when you have finished.

Mrs. Wood : All right.

Nurse : One more thing. We will be getting you out of bed as soon as possible. Perhaps the day after the operation.

** ——————————

urinate〔'jʊrə,net〕*v.* 排尿

✦ Dialogue 2 ✦

Nurse : Have you emptied your bladder?

Mrs. Wood : Yes, I have.

Nurse : Then I would like you to swallow a nasal gastric tube that I have prepared for you.

Mrs. Wood : What is that?

Nurse : ***This N. G. tube*** goes from the nasal cavity to the stomach and ***is attached to a suction motor*** for sucking gastric juice after the operation. Since the digestive system is so affected by the operation and the anesthesia, it will not be functioning well enough and will need a tube to

✦ 實況會話 1 ✦

護　士：手術後，因爲躺著，而且縫口會抽痛，所以排尿有時似乎很困難。試著練習躺在床上排尿，我會把尿盆留在這裡，用好了就告訴我們。

伍德太太：好的。

護　士：還有一件事，我們會儘快讓您下床，或許就在手術的第二天吧。

** ―――――――――――――――

suture〔'sutʃɚ〕*v.*（傷口之）縫口

✦ 實況會話 2 ✦

護　士：您膀胱裡的尿排光了嗎？

伍德太太：是的。

護　士：那麼，請吞下我替您準備的鼻胃管。

伍德太太：那是什麼？

護　士：這支鼻胃管從鼻腔通到胃，連著一部吸引器，手術後用來吸取胃液。因爲手術和痲醉對消化系統影響很大，它不能蠕動得很好，需要一根管子來幫忙排除消化液。您必須等到消化系統恢復正常功能。

assist draining the juice. You have to wait until the digestive system returns to normal functioning.

Mrs. Wood : I see. It seems to be very important, doesn't it?

Nurse : Oh, yes, it is.

** ————————

nasal 〔'nezḷ〕 *adj.* 鼻的
gastric 〔'gæstrɪk〕 *adj.* 胃的

✦ Dialogue 3 ✦

Nurse : I will give you an N.G. tube right now. Will you sit facing me? And (try to) relax.

Mrs. Wood : All right.

Nurse : Do you have any problems with your nasal cavity like deviation or infections?

Mrs. Wood : The membrane of the left nostril seems to be sore sometimes. Will you insert it through the right side?

Nurse : All right. And please try to relax. I am going to insert the tube now. When the tube passes to the entrance of the throat ***you may feel obstructed***, but try to swallow the tube with your saliva. Here it is. Please swallow. Slowly swallow. O.K., stop your swallowing. ***I have aspirated juice which looks like gastric juice*** in the syringe. I will check with the test tape now. Everything is fine. Thank you for your coopera-

伍德太太： 我知道了。好像很重要，不是嗎？

護　士： 噢，是的。

** ————————————————

suction〔'sʌkʃən〕*adj.* 以吸力操作的

✦ 實況會話 3 ✦

護　士： 我馬上給您裝鼻胃管，請面對著我坐好嗎？(試著)放輕鬆。

伍德太太： 好的。

護　士： 您的鼻腔有偏斜或感染的毛病嗎？

伍德太太： 左邊的鼻膜有時會痛。你從右邊插入好嗎？

護　士： 好的，請試著放輕鬆，我現在要插管子了。當管子通過喉嚨入口時，您可能會有被哽住的感覺。但是試著跟唾液吞下去。這就對了。請吞下去，慢慢吞。好，停止吞嚥。注射器裡已經抽出像胃液的消化液了。我現在用試紙來檢驗。一切都很順利，謝謝您的合作。抱歉讓您這麼難受。

tion. I'm sorry I gave you such a hard time.

**

deviation〔,divɪ'eʃən〕*n.* 偏斜

infection〔ɪn'fɛkʃən〕*n.* 感染

membrane〔'mɛmbren〕*n.* 薄膜

✦ Dialogue 4 ✦

Nurse: I will fix the tube with adhesive tape, on the top of the nose and cheek. It will be uncomfortable, but please do not try to remove it. Otherwise you may have problems. This is an important part of the post surgery. Please call a nurse if you have any problems.

Mrs. Wood: How long do I have to keep it?

Nurse: You may have to wait until the bowels start functioning.

Mrs. Wong: I see.

**

adhesive tape 膠布；膠帶

• 字彙備忘欄 •

be attached 連接到…

obstruction〔əb'strʌkʃən〕*n.* 障礙

block〔blɑk〕*v.* 阻塞

aspirate〔'æspə,ret〕*v.*〔醫〕用吸引器將體腔中液體抽出

** ——————————

nostril〔'nɑstrəl〕*n.* 鼻孔
saliva〔sə'laɪvə〕*n.* 唾液
syringe〔'sɪrɪndʒ〕*n.* 注射器

✦ 實況會話 4 ✦

護　士： 我要用膠布把管子固定在鼻子上端和臉頰部位。會很不舒服，但請不要試圖移動它，否則可能會有麻煩。這是外科手術後很重要的一部分，如果有任何問題，請叫護士。

伍德太太： 我這要弄多久呢？

護　士： 可能必須等到腸子開始蠕動。

伍德太太： 我知道了。

** ——————————

bowel〔'baʊəl〕*n.* 腸

● 字彙備忘欄 ●

secretion〔sɪ'kriʃən〕*n.* 分泌物
nutrition〔nju'trɪʃən〕*n.* 營養
dressing〔'drɛsɪŋ〕*n.* 敷藥、繃帶
void〔vɔɪd〕*v.* 排泄

護士必背英語句型

1. ***Urinating after an operation is very hard.***

♧ Passing urine following an operation is usually very difficult.

♧ Voiding after an operation is very hard.

手術後排尿很困難。

2. This tube ***is attached to*** a suction motor.

♧ This tube is connected to the suction machine.

這條管子連到一部吸引器。

3. ***You may feel an obstruction.***

♧ You may feel something like a blocking sensation.

♧ You may have a sensation of obstruction.

您可能會有被哽住的感覺。

4. ***I have aspirated juice which looks like gastric juice.***

♧ I have gotten some secretion which looks like gastric juice. 我已經採到像胃液一樣的消化液了。

LESSON 11

對手術後疼痛的照應

Administering Postoperative Sedation

護士向病患說明服用止痛劑的三種情況。

① 確認止痛劑服用的時間，和答允病人的請求。

② 止痛劑效用短暫時，和醫師商討對策。

③ 有不是因疼痛引起的情緒不穩的狀態時，可服用微量的鎮靜劑。

並告訴病人作深呼吸的方法，及靜脈點滴注射液用完時，請通知護士等等。

✦ Dialogue 1 ✦

Nurse : I saw your light. What can I do for you?

Mrs. Wood : I have so much pain in the wound. I need medicine for (my) pain, nurse.

Nurse : ***Will you show me the dressing? The dressing is clean and dry.*** You had the injections three hours ago, so I think it is about time to give you another pain killer. ***Let me check your blood pressure*** before that.

** ―――――――――――――

dressing〔'drɛsɪŋ〕*n.* 敷藥；綳帶

✦ Dialogue 2 ✦

Nurse : I gave you a pain killer one hour ago. It seems to be a little bit early to give you another one now. This medicine has a very strong effect and the doctor has ordered medication for 2 to 3 hours interval. Can you stand it for a while?

Mrs. Wood : Oh, no, I can't stand it any longer.

Nurse : I see. Then I will call the doctor. Please relax and don't worry.

Mrs. Wood : Please ask him. I would appreciate it.

護　士：我看到您的燈亮了，需要我服務嗎？

伍德太太：護士小姐，我的傷口很痛，需要止痛劑。

護　士：讓我看看繃帶好嗎？繃帶很乾也很乾淨。您在三個鐘頭前打過針，所以我想該給您另一劑止痛針了。在打之前，讓我量量您的血壓。

** ———

pain killer 止痛藥

✦ 實 況 會 話 2 ✦

護　士：我在一個鐘頭前給您止痛了，現在再打止痛針似乎嫌太早。這種藥的藥效很強，而且醫生指示藥物治療要間隔二至三個鐘頭。您能忍耐一下嗎？

伍德太太：噢，不，我不能再忍了。

護　士：哦，那麼我叫醫生來。請放輕鬆，別擔心。

伍德太太：請去問他，我會很感激的。

✦ Dialogue 3 ✦

Nurse : Mrs. Wood, I am afraid you seem to be restless. Can't you sleep or ***does the wound hurt***?

Mrs. Wood : I know it is not hurting but somehow I can't relax.

Nurse : I see. Then, shall I give you a minor sedative? I am sure it will make you more comfortable.

Mrs. Wood : O.K.

** ——————————

sedative〔'sɛdətɪv〕*n.* 鎮定劑

✦ Dialogue 4 ✦

Nurse : ***I think we will have breathing exercises now.*** I will hold your suture site like this. Please take a deep breath like this. In. ……Out. …… In. ……Out. ……Does it hurt?

Mrs. Wood : No.

Nurse : You sound a bit congested in the throat. Will you cough it up? ***I will hold your stomach like this.*** Fine. Then ***please gargle***. Here is the water but do not drink it. Just gargle and I will put this basin by your face. So the water will not run down your neck.

** ——————————

congest〔kən'dʒɛst〕*v.* 充塞

✦ 實況會話 3 ✦

護　士：伍德太太，我看您恐怕似乎很不安，是睡不著，還是傷口疼呢？

伍德太太：我知道那不疼，但是我不知是何緣故，就是不能放輕鬆。

護　士：哦，那麼我給您少量的鎮定劑，好嗎？相信會使您舒服些。

伍德太太：好的。

✦ 實況會話 4 ✦

護　士：我想我們現在來做呼吸運動。我會像這樣按住您的縫口，請像這樣深呼吸，吸……呼……吸……呼……會痛嗎？

伍德太太：不會。

護　士：聽起來您的喉嚨好像有點阻塞，要把它咳出來嗎？我會像這樣按住您的胃。很好，然後請漱口。水在這兒，但不要喝下去。只漱漱口，我會把這盆子擺在您臉旁。這樣水就不會流到脖子去。

** ———

cough up 咳出

✦ Dialogue 5 ✦

Mrs. Wood: Nurse, how long do I have to continue this intravenous injection?

Nurse: You have to keep this injection for a while. Until you can have sufficient nutrition. Well, we will keep an eye on your IV. In case you notice the water level in the bottle has gone down to almost empty or the dripping has stopped or if a back flow of blood can be seen through the IV set tube, please let us know.

Mrs. Wood: Yes, I will.

**

intravenous〔ˌɪntrəˈvinəs〕*adj.* 靜脈注射的（縮寫爲 IV）
nutrition〔njuˈtrɪʃən〕*n.* 營養

● 字彙備忘欄 ●

intact〔ɪnˈtækt〕*adj.* 完整的；無傷的
exercise〔ˈɛksɚˌsaɪz〕*n.* 運動
rinse〔rɪns〕*v.* 清洗
gargle〔ˈgɑrgl〕*v.* 漱口
incision〔ɪnˈsɪʒən〕*n.*〔外科〕切開；割口

✦ 實況會話 5 ✦

伍德太太：護士小姐，我的靜脈內注射得繼續打多久？

護　士：您得打一陣子，直到您獲得足夠的營養。唔，我們會留意您的點滴。如果您注意到瓶子裡，水的高度已經下降到快光了，或是不再滴了，或者如果可以看到固定管裡，有血液回流，請告訴我們。

伍德太太：好的，我會。

** ———

dripping〔'drɪpɪŋ〕*n.* 滴落之物

護士必背英語句型

1. ***Will you show me the dressing***?

♧ May I see the dressing?

♧ May I check the dressing? 讓我看看綳帶好嗎？

2. ***The dressing is clean and dry.***

♧ The dressing is clean and intact.

♧ The dressing is in fine shape. 綳帶很乾也很乾淨。

3. Let me ***check*** your blood pressure.

♧ I would like to ***take*** your blood pressure.

讓我量量您的血壓。

4. ***Does the wound hurt too much***?

♧ Does the incision hurt too much?

♧ Do you have much pain in the incision? 傷口會很痛嗎？

5. I think we will have ***breathing exercises*** now.

♧ I will help you do your breathing exercise now.

我想，我們現在來做呼吸運動。

6. ***I will hold your stomach like this.***

♧ I am going to support your abdomen like this.

♧ I am going to press down your stomach like this.

我會像這樣按住您的胃。

7. ***Please gargle.***

♧ Please wash your mouth.

♧ Please rinse your mouth. 請漱口。

LESSON 12

鼓勵病人手術後儘早下床

Encouraging Early Ambulation

手術後，為了恢復消化器官的機能，應該鼓勵病人儘早下床。

教導病人如何從床上站到地面，如何靠床站穩，如何開始走動，並站在病患床邊幫助她，必要時予以扶持。

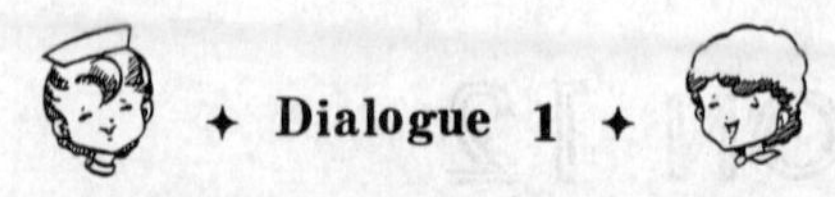

✦ Dialogue 1 ✦

Nurse : How are you feeling today? I notice that the NG tube was removed. I am so glad that you look so relieved.

Mrs. Wood : I feel much better except for the pulling pains when I move.

Nurse : ***You may hear bowel sounds.*** I think your digestive system is ready to start functioning.

Mrs. Wood : I have not passed gas yet. But I can hear the bowel sounds.

** ———

bowel sounds 腹鳴

✦ Dialogue 2 ✦

Nurse : Mrs. Wood, ***it may be hard for you to get out of bed right now.*** But exercising is very important to prevent respiratory complications and promote intestinal functioning as your doctor explained to you.

Mrs. Wood : Walking? Oh, no. I would rather stay still. It hurts so much.

Nurse : I know it hurts when you move. But you will gradually find it easier after the first time. You don't have to worry about the suture. ***Walking does not harm the suture*** at all. I will be glad

護　士：您今天覺得怎麼樣？我注意到鼻胃管已經拿掉了，很高興您看起來這麼舒暢。

伍德太太：除了移動時會抽痛以外，我覺得好多了。

護　士：您可能會聽到腹鳴，我想您的消化系統準備開始蠕動了。

伍德太太：我還沒排氣，但是可以聽到腹鳴。

** ────────

pass gas 排氣

✦ 實況會話 2 ✦

護　士：伍德太太，要您立刻下床可能太難了。但是，正如醫生向您解釋過的，運動對於預防呼吸器官的併發症，以及促進腸胃的蠕動，是非常重要的。

伍德太太：走路嗎？噢，不。我寧可不動，那太痛了。

護　士：我知道移動時會痛，但是您會漸漸發現，第一次以後就比較容易了。您不必擔心縫口，走路一點也不會引起縫口的疼痛。我會很樂意扶您走路。

to help you (to) walk.

Mrs. Wood : Will you hold me?

Nurse : Certainly, Mrs. Wood.

** ——————————

suture 〔'sutʃɚ〕 *n.* (傷口之)縫口

✦ Dialogue 3 ✦

Nurse : Please take time to move by yourself. Bend your knees so as not to pull your stomach muscles. Keep the position and turn toward the side you are going to get out of bed. Please stretch your legs out of bed and try to sit up. ***You will know how to do it best without hurting yourself.*** Please use my shoulder to push yourself out. I will be standing by to assist you. All right. Now, you are standing. All right. You are standing up now. Here are your slippers. Can you put them on slowly?

Mrs. Wood : Yes.

Nurse : How do you feel?

Mrs. Wood : O.K.

Nurse : Please try and stand by holding the IV pole. That's right. Let's walk. Let's try to go to the nurse's station.

伍德太太： 你會扶我嗎？

護　士： 當然，伍德太太。

✦ 實況會話 3 ✦

護　士： 請您自己慢慢移動。彎著膝蓋才不會拉到胃肌，保持這個姿勢，轉向您要下床的那一邊，請把腿伸下床，試著坐直。您知道怎麼做最好，才不會痛。請扶著我的肩膀，站起來。我會站在旁邊協助您。好，現在您要站起來了。好，現在站起來了。您的脫鞋在這兒，您能慢慢穿嗎？

伍德太太： 能。

護　士： 您覺得怎麼樣呢？

伍德太太： 不錯。

護　士： 請試著握住點滴的架子站著。對了。我們走吧，試著走到護士站去。

●字彙備忘欄●

prevent 〔 prɪ'vɛnt 〕 *v*. 預防
respiratory 〔 rɪ'spaɪrə,torɪ 〕 *adj*. 呼吸的
digestive 〔 daɪ'dʒɛstɪv 〕 *adj*. 消化的
complication 〔 ,kɑmplə'keʃən 〕 *n*. 併發症
dizzy 〔 'dɪzɪ 〕 *adj*. 頭昏
incision 〔 ɪn'sɪʒən 〕 *n*. 切口
excision 〔 ɪk'sɪʒən 〕 *n*. 〔外科〕切除
promote 〔 prə'mot 〕 *v*. 促進

《護理重點》

1. 手術後第二天，許多患者怕引起縫口的疼痛，所以躺在床上，一動也不敢動。這時，你應鼓勵病人，試行走動一下，並加以指導，還要注意病人的動作，若有疼痛或不適時，需加以攙扶、協助。
2. 練習走路時，可以告訴病人「我們一塊兒做」，然後在一旁陪病人做練習。
3. 剛開始走路時，得一邊觀察病人的臉色、脈搏、呼吸狀態，尤其是有貧血症狀時，應該特別留心。

護士必背英語句型

1. ***You may hear bowel sounds.***
   ♧ You may hear growling sounds.
   ♧ You may feel a gassy sensation. 您可能會聽到腹鳴。

2. ***It may be hard for you to get out of bed right now.***
   ♧ You may find it hard to walk right now.
   ♧ You may have a hard time in starting to walk now.
   要您立刻下床可能太難了。

3. ***Walking does not harm the suture.***
   ♧ When you walk, you will not hurt the stitches.
   ♧ The stitches won't get hurt by walking.
   走路不會引起縫口的疼痛。

4. ***You will know how to do it best without hurting yourself.***
   ♧ You will find out what is best to do without hurting yourself.
   ♧ You will know how to do what is best without hurting yourself. 您知道怎麼做最好，才不會痛。

LESSON 13

孕婦的電話商議與入院的護理

Consultation over the Telephone and Care for the Pregnant Woman

庫克太太開始陣痛而打電話到醫院。助產護士詢問孕婦疼痛的間隔時間、及預產期，並要她在家等一些時候。

為入院的庫克太太剃毛、灌腸以準備分娩，並將尿杯遞給她，請她採尿化驗。

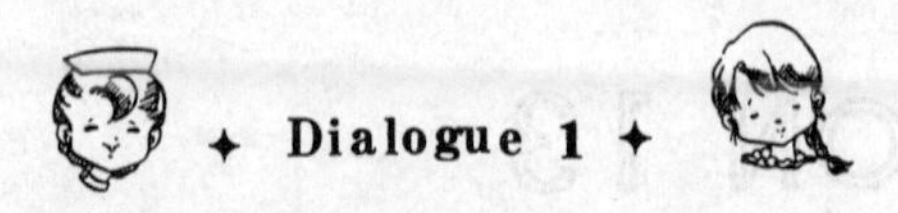

✦ Dialogue 1 ✦

Nurse: Hello, may I help you?

Mrs. Cook: I have a pain from this morning. Am I having labor pain?

Nurse: Is this your first baby? And ***what's the expecting date***?

Mrs. Cook: Yes, this is the first baby and the expecting date is the 30th of April.

Nurse: All right. I want to know how often the contractions are occurring and how long they last.

Mrs. Cook: They started this morning around 9 o'clock and each pain lasts about 10 seconds at intervals of about 20 minutes apart.

Nurse: I see, ***do you have any vaginal discharge***?

Mrs. Cook: Yes, ***it is very thick mucus with a tinge of blood.***

Nurse: It is called a bloody show which is the normal sign. You're in labor now. Are you ready to come to the hospital? How long does it take to come to the hospital?

Mrs. Cook: It takes about 10 minutes.

Nurse: What did the doctor tell you at the last examination? ***Anything other than normal***, like a Caesarian section?

Mrs. Cook: He didn't say anything.

Nurse: Then, you have more time to stay at home, but carefully time your contractions and when the contractions occur every ten minutes and last a

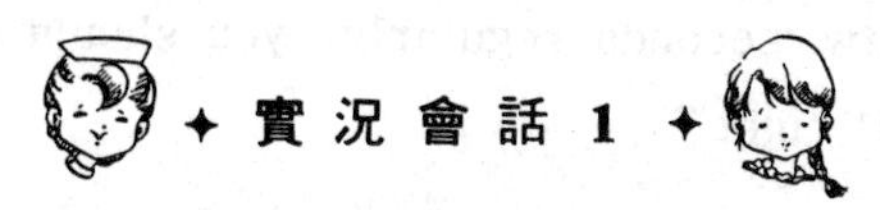

護　士：喂，需要我服務嗎？
庫克太太：我從今天早上開始痛，這是陣痛嗎？

護　士：這是您的頭胎嗎？預產期是哪一天？

庫克太太：是的，這是頭胎，預產期是四月三十日。

護　士：好的。我想知道收縮多久發生一次，每次持續多久。

庫克太太：從今天早上九點左右開始痛的，每次持續十秒左右，間隔約二十分鐘。

護　士：我知道了，您的陰道有任何分泌物嗎？
庫克太太：有，是一種濃稠、帶點血的黏液。
護　士：那叫做現血，是正常現象，您現在要分娩了。準備來醫院了嗎？來醫院要花多少時間？

庫克太太：十分鐘左右。
護　士：上一次檢查時，醫生告訴過您什麼，任何像剖腹生產之類的反常現象嗎？

庫克太太：他沒說什麼。
護　士：那麼，您可以在家待久一點，但是要小心計算收縮的時間，還有，當收縮很規律地每十分鐘發生一次，且持續幾秒鐘時，您應該再打電話給我們，好嗎？

few seconds regularly, you should call us again, all right?

Mrs. Cook: Yes.

Nurse: I need to have your name, age, hospital number, and phone number and please call us if you have watery discharge.

Mrs. Cook: Yes, my name is Mrs. Cook, I am 24 years old, the hospital number is 5766 and my phone number is 623-4568.

** ———

vaginal discharge 陰道分泌物

mucus 〔'mjukəs〕 *n.* (生物) 黏液

✦ Dialogue 2 ✦

Nurse: Good afternoon, Mrs. Cook, We have been waiting for you. Any change since you called us?

Mrs. Cook: I think the contractions are gradually increasing in frequency and intensity.

Nurse: I see, now we will give you preparation for the birth of your baby.

Mrs. Cook: Yes.

Nurse: I will take you to your bed. Come this way, please. You can change into a gown and weigh yourself, please. How much did you gain?

Mrs. Cook: I have gained 9 kilos.

Nurse: That is about the usual gain which is very good.

庫克太太： 好的。

護　士： 我需要知道您的姓名、年齡、病歷號碼和電話號碼，如果您有大量分泌物流出時，請打電話給我們。

庫克太太： 好的，我是庫克太太，二十四歲，病歷號碼是5766，電話號碼是 623-4568 。

** ———

tinge〔tɪndʒ〕*n.* 輕微

Caesarian section 帝王切開術；剖腹生產

✦ 實況會話 2 ✦

護　士： 午安，庫克太太，我們一直在等您來。打電話給我們以來，有任何變化嗎？

庫克太太： 我想收縮的次數和強度逐漸在增加。

護　士： 我知道了，現在我們要替您做接生前的準備工作。

庫克太太： 好的。

護　士： 我帶您到病床，請這邊走。您可以更換長袍，並量體重。您的體重增加了幾公斤？

庫克太太： 增加了九公斤 。

護　士： 那大約是一般孕婦增加的體重，非常好。醫生馬上

The doctor will examine you pretty soon in the examination room, then I will shave the pubic hair and you will have to have an enema. ***We will need a urine sample. Here is a cup.***

** ―――――――――

frequency〔'frikwənsɪ〕*n.* 頻率；次數　enema〔'ɛnəmɑ〕*n.* 灌腸

●字彙備忘欄●

labor〔'lebɚ〕*n.* 分娩；陣痛
expecting date　預產期
contraction〔kən'trækʃən〕*n.* 收縮
bloody show　（分娩時的）現血
intensity〔ɪn'tɛnsətɪ〕*n.* 強度
pretty soon　很快地
pubic hair　陰毛
shaving〔'ʃevɪŋ〕*n.* 剃毛
internal examination　內診
afterbirth〔'æftɚbɝθ〕*n.* 胞衣（胎盤之俗名）
bear down　使勁
primipara〔praɪ'mɪpərə〕*n.* 初產婦
multipara〔mʌl'tɪpərə〕*n.* 多產婦

會在檢查室替您檢查，然後我要剃陰毛，您還得灌

腸。我們需要驗尿，杯子在這裡。

** ———————————

urine〔'jʊrɪn〕 *n.* 尿

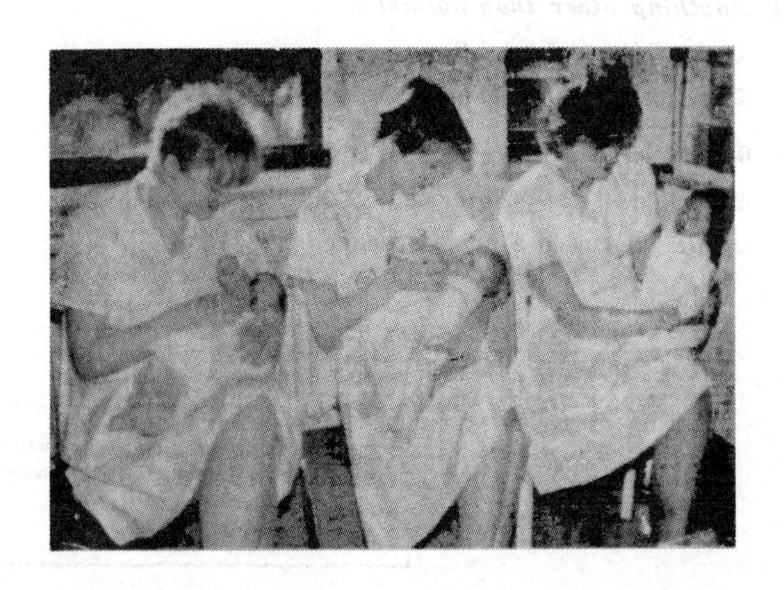

護士必背英語句型

1. ***What is the expecting date*?**
   - ♧ When is your due date?
   - ♧ When are you expecting? 預產期是哪一天?

2. ***Do you have any vaginal discharge*?**
   - ♧ Do you have any discharge from the vagina?
   - ♧ Have you noticed any vaginal discharge?
     您的陰道有任何分泌物嗎?

3. ***It is very thick mucus with a tinge of blood.***
   - ♧ It is very sticky mucus tinged with blood.
   - ♧ It is a discharge with some blood stain.
     是一種濃稠帶點血的黏液。

4. ***Anything other than normal*?**
   - ♧ Anything abnormal?
   - ♧ Something unusual? 有任何反常現象嗎?

5. ***We will need a urine sample.***
   - ♧ We will test your urine.
   - ♧ We will need a urine specimen. 我們需要驗尿。

LESSON 14

婦產科診療室與陣痛室的護理

Obstetric Care in the Labor Room

庫克太太的陣痛越來越強烈。由於病患略顯不安，護士便說些鼓勵她的話，注射促進陣痛劑，並說明理由。在產婦腹部安置聽診器，教導她呼吸法及作背部按摩。

✦ **Dialogue 1** ✦

Nurse : I will check the contractions before shaving. Here come the contractions. ***It lasted*** 20 ***seconds***. The interval is 8 minutes. Please ***bend your knees.*** I will check the fetal position first. Now, I will check the fetal heart beat. So will you stretch your legs please? I will let you hear the heart beat.

Mrs. Cook : Is this normal?

Nurse : Yes, quite normal.

Mrs. Cook : I am afraid I may not be able to cope with the pain.

Nurse : I am sorry but your pain will become progressively worse, but you will be all right. ***Someone will be with you until the baby's birth***. I am now going to shave the pubic hair, so please lie on the examination table. Put your buttocks down to the edge of the table. That's it. I will elevate the table. Please try to relax while shaving, and stop me if you feel uncomfortable.

** ——————————

buttocks 〔'bʌtəks〕 *n.* 臀

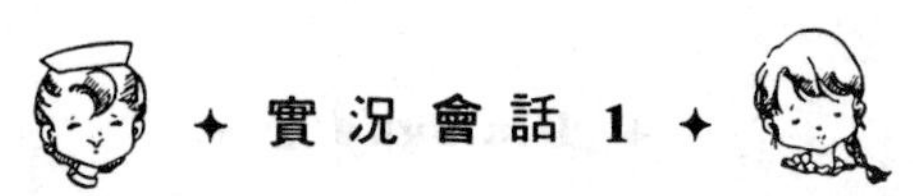

護　士：在剃毛之前，我要檢查收縮的情形。現在收縮了，持續廿秒鐘，間隔是八分鐘。請把膝蓋彎起來，我要先檢查胎兒的位置。現在，我要聽聽胎兒的心跳，所以請您把腿伸直，好嗎？我讓您聽聽心跳。

庫克太太：這樣正常嗎？

護　士：是的，相當正常。

庫克太太：我怕克服不了疼痛。

護　士：很遺憾，但是您會越來越痛，不過您會很順利的。有人會陪著您，直到嬰兒出生。我現在要剃陰毛了，所以，請您躺在檢查台上，臀部放在台子的邊緣，就是這樣。我把台子升高。當我在剃的時候，請試著放輕鬆，如果您覺得不舒服，就叫我停下來。

✦ Dialogue 2 ✦

Mrs. Cook： When will I have my baby?

Nurse： I think possibly before midnight. I've finished shaving. I am going to give you the enema next. **Take a deep breath, breathing through your mouth,** and relax. I will put the table down. Let me help you to get off the table. Come this way. Please call me if you have any trouble. Here is the emergency button. I need to check the bowel movement, so don't flush the toilet.

Mrs. Cook： Yes.

Nurse： Now you're ready to go to the labor room. I will take you there, then, ***you can see your husband.***

Mrs. Cook： I want my husband to stay with me in the labor room and during the delivery. Will that be all right?

Nurse： Yes. ***We were notified*** by the doctor that you want your husband to be with you during the delivery.

Mrs. Cook： Thank you.

** ———

labor room　分娩室

✦ 實況會話 2 ✦

庫克太太：我的小孩什麼時候生出來？

護　士：我想大概在午夜以前。我已經剃好了。接下來，要給您灌腸，作一次深呼吸，用嘴巴呼吸，放鬆。我要把台子降下來，我來扶您下來，請走這邊。如果有什麼事，請叫我。這是緊急按扭。我必須檢查腸子蠕動的情形，所以，排便後請不要冲掉。

庫克太太：好的。

護　士：現在，您準備到分娩室去，我帶您去，那時候您就可以看到您先生了。

庫克太太：我要我先生在分娩室及生產時陪著我，可以嗎？

護　士：可以的。醫生已通知我們，說您生產時，要先生陪著。

庫克太太：謝謝你。

✦ Dialogue 3 ✦

Nurse: Mrs. Cook, the doctor has ordered to induce the labor, so I will give you an injection. And the effect should be kept until the placenta delivery.

Mrs. Cook: Does that mean increasing the contractions and frequency?

Nurse: Yes, it will hasten the delivery. You are going to stay here until the cervix is fully dilated.

Mrs. Cook: Yes.

Nurse: I will set the monitor on your abdomen to check the fetal heart beat and intensity of the contraction.

Mrs. Cook: This backache is killing me.

Nurse: I will massage your back. You can push the back with your thumbs yourself and you can continue to try mouth-breathing.

** ——————

induce〔ɪn'djus〕*v*. 誘發；惹起

placenta〔plə'sɛntə〕*n*.〔動物, 解剖〕胎盤

cervix〔'sɝvɪks〕*n*.〔解剖〕子宮頸

✦ 實況會話 3 ✦

護　士：庫克太太，醫生指示要誘發陣痛，所以我要幫您打一針，藥效應該會持續到胎盤剝離。

庫克太太：那就是說增加收縮和次數嗎？

護　士：是的。那會加速生產，您要待在這裡直到子宮頸全開。

庫克太太：好的。

護　士：我把聽診器放在您的下腹，來檢查胎兒的心跳，和收縮的強度。

庫克太太：我的背痛死了！

護　士：我來按摩您的背部。您可以自已用姆指推背，而且，可以繼續試著用口呼吸。

** ────────────

dilate〔daɪ'let〕*v*. 擴張
monitor〔'mɑnətɚ〕*n*. 聽診器；檢音器
abdomen〔'æbdəmən〕*n*. 下腹

● 字彙備忘備 ●

interval〔'ɪntəvḷ〕*n.* 間隔
fetal heart beat 胎兒心跳聲
examination table 檢查台
birth canal 產道
basal body temperature 基礎體溫
fetal movement 胎動
rupture of membrane 薄膜破裂；破水

《護理重點》

1. 因應檢查所需，而要求產婦調整身體或姿勢時，應於一旁伶巧地協助。
2. 用聽診器，讓產婦聽聽嬰兒心跳的聽音，可減少產婦的焦慮。
3. 指導呼吸法，一方面也能鼓勵產婦，增加不少助力。

護士必背英語句型

1. ***It lasted* 20 *seconds.***
   ♧ It continued 20 seconds.
   ♧ It was 20 seconds long. 它持續了二十秒。

2. ***Bend your knees.***
   ♧ Draw your knees up.
   ♧ Bring your knees up. 把膝蓋打彎。

3. ***Someone will be with you until the baby's birth.***
   ♧ Someone will be with you through the delivery.
   ♧ Somebody will stay with you during the delivery.
   有人會陪著您直到嬰兒出生。

4. ***You can see your husband.*** 您就看得到您先生了。
   ♧ Your husband will be there. 您先生會在那裡。
   ♧ Your husband is waiting there. 您先生正在那裡等。

5. ***We were notified.*** 我們已經得到通知。
   ♧ We already know about.
   ♧ We have been told. 我們已經知道了。

LESSON 15

產房內及生產後的護理

Delivery Care and Postpartum Care

終於要開始生產了。護士將庫克太太移到分娩台上。向她說明脚的位置和用力的部位，再指導她正確的呼吸方法。生下了小孩，護士說：「恭禧，是個男孩。」將小孩抱給庫克太太。

生產後，指導產婦對自己和嬰兒的正確護理方式。

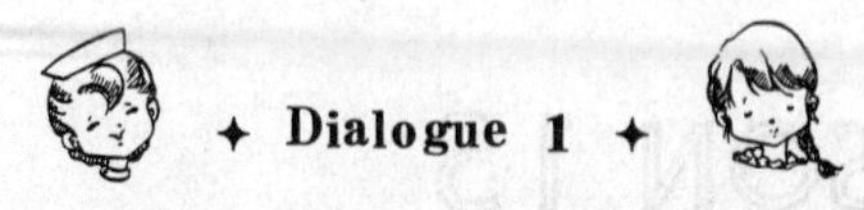

✦ Dialogue 1 ✦

Nurse : Mrs. Cook, you are ready to go to the delivery room. Your husband will be with you.

Mrs. Cook : Yes.

Nurse : Please move to the delivery table. It's better to put your buttocks on the table first, and put your feet in the stirrups please.

Mrs. Cook : Oh, the contractions are coming. I can't bear it anymore.

Nurse : Take a deep breath …… good, then exhale slowly. You can grip the hand grips. It may help you. It won't be long now. It's progressing very well. ***Please do as I say.*** O.K.? Now, take a deep breath and hold it …… good. Then ***bear down*** …… good. Take another breath. Push down again. You are doing fine. Take a short breath. Your baby has come. Mrs. Cook, you have a beautiful baby boy. Congratulations!

Mrs. Cook : Thank you. I'm very happy.

Nurse : Would you like to hold your baby for a while?

Mrs. Cook : Yes, please.

護　士：庫克太太，您即將到接生室去，您先生會陪著您。

庫克太太：好的。

護　士：請到接生台上，最好臀部先坐上去，請把脚放在鐙子裡。

庫克太太：噢！收縮又來了！我再也忍不住了。

護　士：深呼吸……很好，然後慢慢呼氣。您可以抓住手把，這樣會有幫助。現在快了，進行得很順利，請照我說的做，好嗎？現在，深呼吸，彆住氣……很好。然後使勁……很好。再吸一口氣，再使勁些，您做得很好。淺淺地吸一口氣，您的小孩出來了。庫克太太，您生了一個漂亮的小男孩。恭禧您！

庫克太太：謝謝你，我很高興。

護　士：您想要抱一下小孩子嗎？

庫克太太：好的

✦ Dialogue 2 ✦

Nurse : Did you sleep well? I will check the fundus of the uterus and see how it's contracted. Then let me check the perineal pads for the amount of lochia. If everything is O.K., you can walk to the toilet with me.

Mrs. Cook : Yes.

Nurse : I will show you how to care for the perineal area yourself. You should wipe the perineum from the top toward the rectum with the clean wet wiper. This is important, then take another wiper to clean the other side. You may need to repeat this ***several times***. Do you understand this procedure?

Mrs. Cook : Yes.

** ―――――――――――――

lochia〔'lαkɪə〕*n.*〔醫〕惡露；產褥排泄物

rectum〔'rɛktəm〕*n.*〔解剖〕直腸

✦實況會話 2 ✦

護　士：您睡得好嗎？我要檢查子宮的底部，看它收縮得怎樣。然後，讓我檢查會陰墊上惡露的數量。如果一切順利的話，您可以和我走到厠所去。

庫克太太：好的。

護　士：我要教您怎樣自己料理會陰部。您應該用乾淨的溼布擦會陰，從頂部擦向直腸的部位。這是很重要的，然後，拿另一塊布，把其他部位擦乾淨，您可能必須重覆好幾次。了解這項程序嗎？

庫克太太：了解。

** ———

perineum〔,pɛrə'niəm〕*n.*〔解剖〕會陰

✦ Dialogue 3 ✦

Nurse: Here is your baby. ***He looks like his father.*** Would you like ***to nurse him***?

Mrs. Cook: Yes, I will.

Nurse: Can I see your breast? Can you see if there's milk coming?

Mrs. Cook: Yes, can I nurse him?

Nurse: Yes, you hold the baby with your arm, and with the other hand you hold the breast to keep the nipple in his mouth. Try to put the baby's tongue under the nipple, so he can suck well.

Mrs. Cook: He is sucking very well.

Nurse: Usually it takes a few days before you will have enough milk. In order to produce milk, the sucking stimulus by the baby is necessary. You may feel the contraction of the uterus while the baby is nursing, which is very normal. This is the sign that the uterus is returning to normal.

** ———

nipple 〔'nɪpl̩〕 *n.* 乳頭

✦實況會話 3✦

護　士：這是您的嬰兒，他看起來像父親，您要餵他母乳嗎?

庫克太太：是的，我要。

護　士：我可以看看您的乳房嗎？您看得到是否有乳汁流出來呢？

庫克太太：有的，我可以餵他母乳嗎？

護　士：可以，您用手臂抱住嬰兒，用另一隻手握住乳房，把乳頭放在他的嘴裏。試著把嬰兒的舌頭，擺在乳頭下，這樣他可以吸得很好。

庫克太太：他吸得很好。

護　士：通常要等幾天您才有足夠的乳汁。爲了產乳，嬰兒吸吮的刺激是必要的。當嬰兒在吸乳時，您或許會感到子宮在收縮，這是很正常的。是子宮恢復正常的跡象。

** ――――――――――

suck〔sʌk〕*v.* 吸吮

●字彙備忘欄●

delivery table 接生台
buttocks〔'bʌtəks〕*n.* 臀部
stirrups〔'stɝəps〕*n.* 脚鐙
exhale〔ɪg'zel〕*v.* 呼氣
nurse〔nɝs〕*v.* 哺乳
short breath 短促的呼吸
fundus of uterus 子宮底部
stimulus〔'stɪmjələs〕*n.* 刺激
laceration of perineum 會陰裂傷
colostrum〔kə'lɑstrəm〕*n.* 初乳
meconium〔mə'konɪəm〕*n.* 胎糞

護士必背英語句型

1. ***Please do as I say.***
   - ♧ Please do what I say.
   - ♧ Please do what I tell you. 請照我說的做。
2. ***Bear down.***
   - ♧ Push down.
   - ♧ Keep pushing. 使勁。
3. ***several times***
   - ♧ a few times
   - ♧ two or three times 好幾次
4. ***He looks like his father.***
   - ♧ He takes after his father.
   - ♧ He resembles his father. 他看起來像父親。
5. ***to nurse him***
   - ♧ to give him breast milk
   - ♧ to give him mother's milk 餵他母乳

LESSON 16

小孩住院時與母親的談話

Conversation with the Mother of a Sick Child

章伯太太的女兒住院了，護士向母親打聽她的女兒貝絲日常的生活習慣。由於對方很擔心女兒的情況，護士便勸慰她不必擔心，並親切地和小貝絲打招呼。

✦ Dialogue 1 ✦

Nurse : How are you, Mrs. Webb? ***What is the problem with your daughter***? Hi, dear!

Mrs. Webb : She fell down the stairway and hit her head, I suppose. I wasn't there at that time. Her ankle has been cracked, too.

Nurse : I will take your daughter and get her into bed and you can tell me about her and what has happened.

Mrs. Webb : Yes.

Nurse : Her name is Elizabeth Webb. ***What do you call her at home***?

Mrs. Webb : We call her Beth.

Nurse : So we should call her Beth in the hospital.

✦ Dialogue 2 ✦

Nurse : Does Beth wake up during the night for the toilet? If she does, what time is that?

Mrs. Webb : Yes, usually she wakes up around 2 o'clock.

Nurse : All right. We can help Beth to go to the toilet or if she needs, we can give her a bed pan to use. Has she any brothers and sisters?

Mrs. Webb : Yes, she has two elder brothers who are 10 and 13 years old. She is the youngest one.

Nurse : Has she had measles, chickenpox or any other diseases?

✦ 實況會話 1 ✦

護　士：您好嗎？韋伯太太。您的女兒怎麼了？嗨，小可愛!

韋伯太太：我想她是從樓梯上摔下來，撞到頭部。當時我不在場。她的脚踝也裂了。

護　士：我帶您的女兒到床上去躺著，您再告訴我關於她的事，以及發生的事情。

韋伯太太：好的。

護　士：她的姓名是伊莉莎白・韋伯。您們在家裡怎麼叫她呢？

韋伯太太：我們叫她貝絲。

護　士：那麼在醫院裡，我們應該叫她貝絲。

✦ 實況會話 2 ✦

護　士：貝絲半夜會醒來上厠所嗎？假如會，是在什麼時候呢？

韋伯太太：會，她通常在兩點左右醒過來。

護　士：好的。我們會幫助貝絲上厠所，或者如果她需要，我們可以給她一個便盆，讓她使用。她有兄弟姊妹嗎？

韋伯太太：有，她有兩個哥哥，一個十歲，一個十三歲。她是老么。

護　士：她得過痲疹、水痘或其他任何的疾病嗎？

Mrs. Webb : Yes, she had most of the children's diseases already.

Nurse : Has she any food likes and dislikes? And what are her favorite foods?

Mrs. Webb : She eats almost anything, even Chinese food.

Nurse : That's good. Is there a particular toy she needs to have? If it's not very large, she can have it with her.

Mrs. Webb : She must have a small blue colored blanket with her when she sleeps.

Nurse : Oh, yes, Beth can have it.

** ―――――――――――――

measles〔'mizḷz〕*n.* 痲疹

✦ Dialogue 3 ✦

Nurse : ***Do you have any questions to ask***? Please don't hesitate to ask us anything.

Mrs. Webb : May I stay with her tonight?

Nurse : I am afraid to say that you can not stay overnight. You may stay until Beth falls asleep. I know how you feel leaving the child behind you.

Mrs. Webb : Yes, I understand. Can I phone early tomorrow morning to know her condition?

Nurse : Certainly, Mrs. Webb. We will take care of her very carefully, please try not to worry.

Mrs. Webb : Yes.

韋伯太太：有，大多數小孩的疾病她都已經得過了。

護　士：她會偏食嗎？什麼是她最喜愛的食物呢？

韋伯太太：她幾乎任何食物都吃，連中國菜也吃。

護　士：那很好。她需要有特別的玩具嗎？假如不太大，她可以帶在身邊。

韋伯太太：她睡覺時，必須要蓋一條藍色的小毯子。

護　士：噢，是的，貝絲可以帶來。

** ———

chickenpox〔tʃɪkən,pɑks〕*n.* 水痘

✦ 實況會話 3 ✦

護　士：您有什麼問題要問嗎？請不要猶豫，儘管問。

韋伯太太：我今晚可以留下來陪她嗎？

護　士：我恐怕得說，您不能留下來過夜。您可以留到貝絲入睡，我了解您把小孩子留下來的心情。

韋伯太太：是的，我知道。我明天一大早可以打電話來了解她的情況嗎？

護　士：當然可以，韋伯太太。我們會很細心地照顧她，請別擔心。

韋伯太太：好的。

Nurse : Beth needs to have bed rest for a while and we should be observing her. If she has any pain, she can tell us, can't she?

Mrs. Webb : Yes, she can.

Nurse : As the doctor has told you, her left ankle will have to be in a cast.

Mrs. Webb : Yes. When will this take place?

Nurse : This afternoon.

● 字彙備忘欄 ●

ankle 〔 'æŋkl̩ 〕 *n.* 脚踝
bed pan 便盆
crack 〔 kræk 〕 *v.* 破裂
favorite food 最喜愛的食物
sprain 〔 spren 〕 *v.* 扭傷
inflammation 〔 ,ɪnflə'meʃən 〕 *n.* 發炎
redness 〔 'rɛdnɪs 〕 *n.* 紅
swelling 〔 'swɛlɪŋ 〕 *n.* 腫
induration 〔 ,ɪndjʊ'reʃən 〕 *n.* 硬化
dislocation 〔 ,dɪslo'keʃən 〕 *n.* 脫臼
traction 〔 'trækʃən 〕 *n.* （肌肉、器官等之）牽引

護　士： 貝絲暫時必須在床上休養，我們將會觀察她的情況。如果痛的話，她會告訴我們，不是嗎？

韋伯太太： 是的，她會。

護　士： 正如醫生告訴過您的，她的左脚踝得上石膏。

韋伯太太： 是的，什麼時候上石膏呢？

護　士： 今天下午。

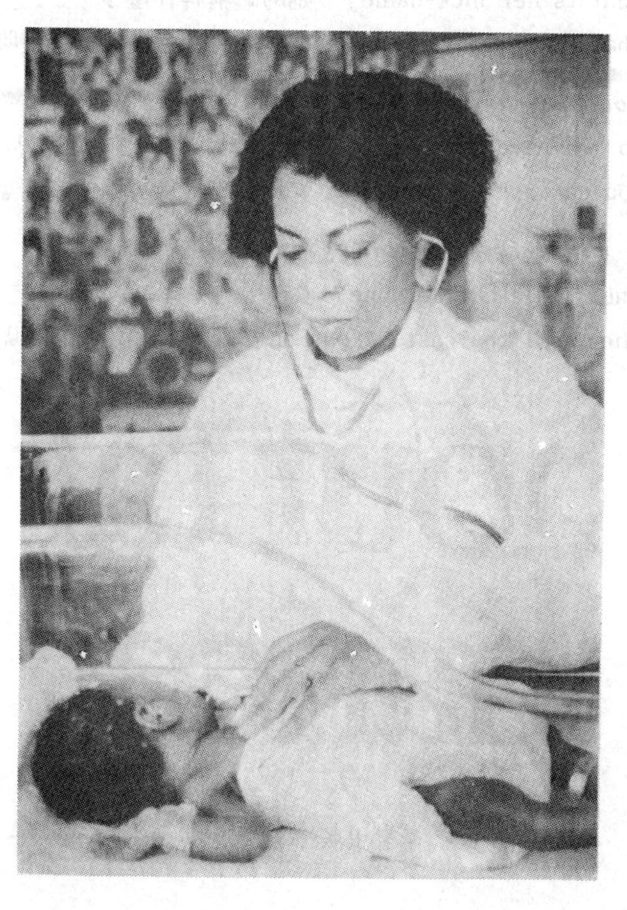

護士必背英語句型

1. ***What is the problem with Beth?***
   - ♧ What is the matter with Beth?
   - ♧ What happened to Beth? 貝絲怎麼了？

2. ***What do you call her at home?*** 您們在家裡怎麼叫她呢？
   - ♧ What is her nick-name? 她的暱稱叫什麼？
   - ♧ What does she like to be called? 她喜歡人家怎麼叫她呢？

3. ***Do you have any questions to ask?***
   - ♧ Do you have anything to ask? 有什麼問題要問嗎？
   - ♧ You can ask anything you want to. 您可以儘量問。

4. ***When will this take place?***
   - ♧ When will that be done?
   - ♧ When will the cast be put on? 什麼時候要上石膏呢？

LESSON 17

對小兒科病患的住院護理

Admission Care for the Pediatric Patient

護士對小病人說可以在床上使用便器，為了讓小孩子懂得這個道理，還得細心地哄她。

摸她的脚使她感覺疼痛，藉機告訴她，接受醫生的治療就不疼了。

為減輕孩子的恐懼，可以用一些坐輪椅散步、在石膏上繪畫的有趣話題，加以誘導。

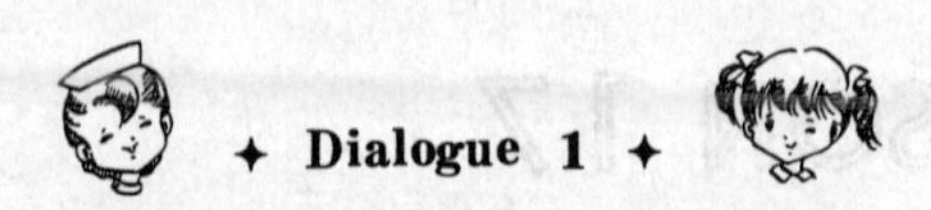

✦ Dialogue 1 ✦

Nurse: Hi, Beth. What are you doing? Oh, you can fold the paper. You are good at it.

Beth: This is supposed to be a bird.

Nurse: Yes, I can see that. Do you hurt any place today?

Beth: No.

Nurse: So you don't want to lie in the bed, do you? Beth, do you want to go to the toilet? Let's try the bed pan.

Beth: ***How can I pee in bed?***

Nurse: Well, I will help you. Can you see the little girl over there? She is using the bed pan. You will be a good girl too, won't you? Because walking will hurt your ankle very much, it is better to use the bed pan for a while.

Beth: Will you help me?

Nurse: Surely, Beth, I will stay with you, good girl.

** ———————————

bed pan 便盆

護　士：嗨，貝絲。你在做什麼？噢，你會摺紙，你很會摺嘛。

貝　絲：這摺起來是一隻鳥。

護　士：是的，看得出來。你今天有哪裡痛嗎？

貝　絲：沒有。

護　士：所以你不想躺在床上，是嗎？貝絲，你想上厠所嗎？用便盆試試看吧。

貝　絲：我要怎樣才能在床上小便呢？

護　士：唔，我會幫你的。你看得到那邊的小女孩嗎？她正在使用便盆。你也要做好孩子，不是嗎？因為，走路會把脚踝弄得很痛，所以你最好暫時使用便盆。

貝　絲：你會幫我嗎？

護　士：當然囉，貝絲，我會在這裡陪你的，好孩子。

✦ Dialogue 2 ✦

Nurse: Beth, let me see your ankle, please. Oh, ***it is swollen a bit***. Does it hurt you?

Beth: Yes!

Nurse: The doctor will take care of your ankle. We are going to put a cast on your ankle. Don't worry. After the cast is on, your ankle will not hurt you any more.

Beth: I don't want to. I'm scared. It hurts.

Nurse: Don't be scared. I am always beside you. After that I will take you on a ride to the roof to see many birds. Won't that be nice?

Beth: I can't walk.

Nurse: I will put you in the wheelchair. Have you ever ridden in a wheelchair before?

Beth: No.

Nurse: ***It might be fun***. Don't you think so, Beth?

Beth: I'll go, but please don't hurt me, promise me?

Nurse: Sure, Beth. We promise not to hurt you. I will take you to another room. ***Do you want to have your blanket***?

Beth: Yes, my blanket please.

** ————————————

swell〔swɛl〕*v.* 發腫

✦ 實況會話 2 ✦

護　士：貝絲，請讓我看看你的脚踝。噢，有一點腫，會痛嗎？

貝　絲：會！

護　士：醫生會照料你的脚踝。我們要把你的脚踝裹上石膏，別擔心，上了石膏以後，脚踝就不會再痛了。

貝　絲：我不要，我害怕，會痛。

護　士：別害怕，我會一直陪著你。上石膏以後，我會用坐椅推你到頂樓上，去看許多小鳥。那不是很好嗎？

貝　絲：我不能走路。

護　士：我會把你放在輪椅上。你以前曾經坐過輪椅嗎？

貝　絲：沒有。

護　士：那可能很有趣，你不認爲嗎，貝絲？

貝　絲：我要去，但是請別弄痛我，答不答應？

護　士：當然了，貝絲。我們保證不弄痛你。我帶你到另一個房間。你要帶你的毯子去嗎？

貝　絲：要，請把毯子拿給我。

** ______

wheelchair〔ˈwhilˈtʃɛr〕*n.* 輪椅

✦ Dialogue 3 ✦

Nurse: Beth, lie on the table. Don't be scared. You're going to be all right. Here is the long white bandage. Can you see? We are going to wrap your ankle, so it will not hurt you any more. If you want to hold me, you can. See, Beth. It doesn't hurt.

Beth: No!

Nurse: It's all finished, Beth. You have been a good girl. You can paint on the cast when it's dried. Your mummy can even sign on it.

Beth: Can I? Won't it hurt me?

Nurse: No, it won't hurt you any more. You can write what you want and paint it, too. I will tell your mummy how good you were. You can tell her yourself, too.

Beth: When can I walk?

Nurse: The doctor will tell you when you can walk. Until that time you will stay in bed and put your leg on a pillow. But you can play with your toys and other things.

** ———

bandage〔'bændɪdʒ〕*n.* 绷帶

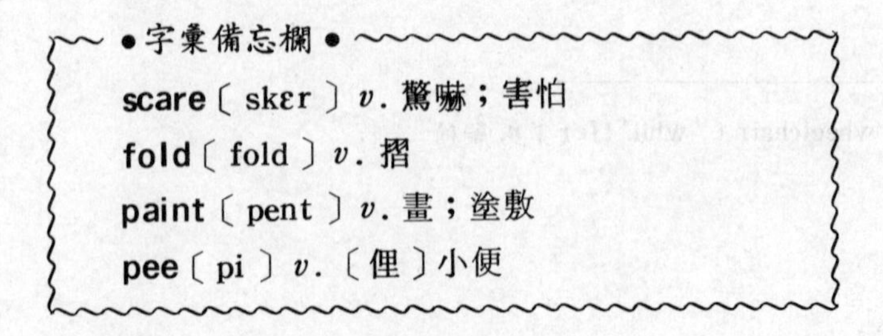
●字彙備忘欄●

scare〔skɛr〕*v.* 驚嚇；害怕

fold〔fold〕*v.* 摺

paint〔pent〕*v.* 畫；塗敷

pee〔pi〕*v.*〔俚〕小便

✦實況會話 3 ✦

護　士：貝絲，躺在台上，別怕。你會好的。這是長的白綳帶，看到了嗎？我們要把你的脚踝包起來，這樣它就不會再痛了。如果你要的話，可以抓著我。看吧，貝絲，不痛的。

貝　絲：不要！

護　士：都弄好了，貝絲。你是個好孩子。等石膏乾了以後，你可以在上面畫畫。你媽咪甚至可以在上面簽名。

貝　絲：可以嗎？那不會痛嗎？

護　士：不會的，它再也不會痛了。你想寫什麼都可以，也可以畫畫。我會告訴你媽咪你有多乖，你也可以自己告訴她。

貝　絲：我什麼時候可以走路呢？

護　士：醫生會告訴你什麼時候可以走路。直到那時候，你都得待在床上，把脚放在枕頭上。但是，你可以玩玩具或別的東西。

●字彙備忘欄●

night-terrors 夜驚

convulsion〔 kən'vʌlʃən 〕*n.*〔醫〕痙攣

weaning diet 斷乳後的食物

infant〔 'ɪnfənt 〕*n.* 嬰兒

護士必背英語句型

1. ***How can I pee in bed?***

♧ How can I urinate in bed?

♧ How can I tinkle in bed? 我怎樣才能在床上小便呢？

2. ***It is swollen a bit.***

♧ You have a slightly swollen ankle.

♧ It is swollen a little. 它有點腫。

3. ***It might be fun.***

♧ It might be an exciting thing.

♧ It might be amusing. 那可能很有趣。

4. ***Do you want to have your blanket?***

♧ Do you want to keep your blanket with you?
你要帶你的毯子去嗎？

♧ You can take your blanket with you if you wish.
如果你要的話，你可以帶你的毯子。

LESSON 18

急診室的資料收集

Information Gathering at the Emergency Room

急診室的護士趕緊出來迎接救護車送來的伍德先生，患者說心痛得很厲害，似乎非常嚴重。

護士小姐機智地採取一些緊急措施，並詢問病患有關的資料。

再詳細地向病人家屬探詢病況和經過。

一會兒之後，受到醫師指示將病患送入CCU室。

Nurse : Mr. Wood, we will move you from the stretcher to this bed. Here you are. Would you mind rolling over? I will help you. Thank you. I am going to ***put your head up*** a little bit higher so you will be able to breathe more easily. Is that better?

Mr. Wood : Yes.

Nurse : Do you have much pain, Mr. Wood?

Mr. Wood : Yes, here. Very sharp (one).

Nurse : I see. Let me take your blood pressure. ***When did this pain start***?

Mr. Wood : Almost 2 hours ago.

Nurse : I see. Did you take any medicine for it?

Mr. Wood : I took nitroglycerin ***under the tongue***. But ***it didn't help*** at all.

Nurse : I see. The doctor will see you now and we will take an ECG immediately. Mr. Wood, please ***don't move*** while we take your ECG.

** ———

stretcher〔ˈstrɛtʃɚ〕*n.* 擔架

nitroglycerin〔ˌnaɪtrəˈglɪsrɪn〕*n.*〔化〕硝酸甘油

護　士：伍德先生，我們要將您從擔架移到這張床上。移好了。您介意轉過身來嗎？我來幫您。謝謝。我要把您的頭墊高一點，這樣您比較好呼吸。這樣好些了嗎？

伍德先生：是的。

護　士：伍德先生，很痛嗎？

伍德先生：是的，這裡。痛死了。

護　士：我知道了，讓我量量您的血壓。什麼時候開始痛的?

伍德先生：大約兩個鐘頭以前。

護　士：我知道了。您吃過什麼藥嗎？

伍德先生：我把硝酸甘油片含在舌頭下，但是一點也沒有用。

護　士：我知道了。醫生現在要看您，我們立刻照心電圖。伍德先生，當我們照心電圖的時候，請不要移動。

** ————

ECG = electrocardiogram〔ɪ'lɛktro'kɑdrə,græm〕*n.*〔醫〕心電圖

✦ Dialogue 2 ✦

Nurse : Excuse me, ***are you related to Mr. Wood***?

Mrs. Wood : Yes, I'm his wife.

Nurse : I see. ***Will you tell me about his illness***?

Mrs. Wood : Yes. He has angina. Once in a while he has chest pain and he gets very uncomfortable. He did not feel good all day yesterday. And he woke up with severe pain at 2 o'clock in the morning. He took one tablet of nitroglycerin right away, but it did not relieve the pain. So he took another tablet about 20 minutes later. Yet he did not feel any better. Soon he became restless and he seemed to have a hard time breathing. So I called up the hospital and we came straight here.

Nurse : When was he diagnosed as having angina?

Mrs. Wood : Two months ago. But he never has had this kind of pain.

Nurse : Thank you, I understand. Mrs. Wood, we will take your husband to the ***coronary care unit*** for some treatment. Will you come along with us?

Mrs. Wood : Yes, I will.

** ———

angina〔æn'dʒaɪnə〕*n.*〔醫〕狹心症；心絞痛症

✦ 實況會話 2 ✦

護　士：對不起，請問您是伍德先生的家屬嗎？

伍德太太：是的，我是他太太。

護　士：我知道了。您能告訴我有關他的症狀嗎？

伍德太太：好的。他有狹心症，偶而胸部會疼痛，變得很不舒服。他昨天一整天都不舒服，今天早上兩點因爲劇痛而醒過來，就馬上含了一片硝酸甘油，但是疼痛並沒有減輕。所以大約二十分鐘後，他又服了一片，然而還是沒感覺舒服些。他不久就變得很煩躁，呼吸也似乎很困難，所以我就打電話給醫院，直接到這裡來了。

護　士：什麼時候診斷出他有狹心症呢？

伍德太太：兩個月以前。但是他從來沒像這樣痛過。

護　士：謝謝您，我了解了。伍德太太，我們要把您先生帶到冠狀動脈集中治療室，做一些治療。您要跟著去嗎？

伍德太太：是的，我要去。

** ———————————

coronary〔ˈkɔrəˌnɛrɪ〕*adj.*〔解剖〕冠狀的

● 字彙備忘欄 ●

ambulance〔'æmbjələns〕*n*. 救護車
onset of the illness 發病
key person 家中之主
local medical doctor 就近的醫生
consulting room 診察室
restless〔'rɛstlɪs〕*adj*. 不穩定的；不寧的
specific details 明確的細節
injury〔'ɪndʒərɪ〕*n*. 傷害
doctor on call 値班醫生

《護理重點》

1. 急診室本來就是氣氛比較緊張的地方，適當的微笑、親切的語氣，都能減少病人的不安。
2. 拐彎抹角的詢問隨侍病人左右的人是誰，有損病人的尊嚴，還是大大方方，直接了當的問「你們是什麼關係？」比較好。
3. 要記錄詢問資料時，常用的說法，例如「請談談他的病況」等等。

護士必背英語句型

1. ***Please put your head up.***
   ♧ Lift your head up, please.
   ♧ Please pull your head up. 請把頭抬起來。

2. ***When did this pain start?***
   ♧ When did you first feel pain?
   ♧ When did the pain begin? 什麼時候開始痛的？

3. ***Put this capsule under your tongue.***
   ♧ Place this capsule under your tongue.
   ♧ This capsule goes under your tongue. 把這膠囊含在舌頭下。

4. ***It did not help the pain.***
   ♧ It did not subside the pain.
   ♧ It did not relieve the pain. 那不能止痛。

5. ***Don't move, please.***
   ♧ Stay still, please.
   ♧ Keep still, please. 請不要動。

6. ***Are you related to him?*** 您是他的家屬嗎？
   ♧ How are you related to him? 您和他是什麼關係呢？
   ** 這兩句話稍有差異，通常以第一句的說法較恰當。

7. ***Will you tell me about his illness?***
   ♧ Could you tell me about his illness?
   ♧ Will you explain his illness to me?
   您能告訴我有關他的病症嗎？

LESSON 19

在CCU的護理

Administering Treatment at CCU(Coronary Care Unit)

CCU的護士要為伍德先生進行緊急治療，請病人家屬在外面等候，隨即開始行動。先從鎖骨下的靜脈測定中心靜脈的血壓，同時進行靜脈點滴注射，插入導尿管，使用鎮定劑等等，然後知會病人家屬。

由醫師向病人家屬説明患者的狀況，並請她辦理住院手續。

✦ Dialogue 1 ✦

Nurse: Mrs. Wood, ***will you please wait outside the room for a while***? We would like to do some treatment.

Mrs. Wood: O. K.

Nurse: Mr. Wood, here is oxygen. It will help you a lot. ***I'm going to apply patches for the monitor on your chest***, so we can see your heart condition from the monitor.

Mr. Wood: I see.

Nurse: Your doctor is going to place an intravenous catheter in your neck vein to check the blood volume of the heart, and also to give you medicine. O. K.?

Mr. Wood: Yes.

Nurse: Please turn your head to the right. ***I'm going to clean the area with tincture*** and the doctor will give you a local anesthetic injection. You may feel a slight pain.

Mr. Wood: All right.

** ——————————

intravenous 〔,ɪntrə'vinəs〕 *adj.* 〔醫〕靜脈的

catheter 〔'kæθɪtɚ〕 *n.* 〔醫〕導管

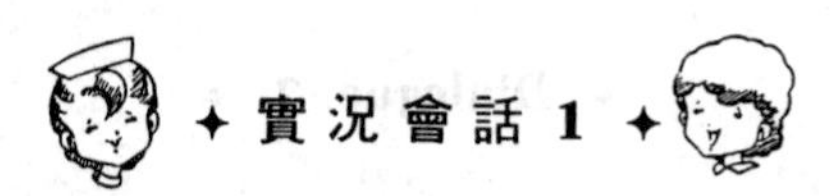

護　士： 伍德太太，請在房外等一會兒好嗎？我們要做一些治療。

伍德太太： 好的。

護　士： 伍德先生，這是氧氣，對您會有很大的幫助。我要把探測器的膠布貼在您的胸部，這樣我們可以從探測器看到您心臟的情況。

伍德先生： 我知道了。

護　士： 醫生要在您的頸部靜脈上裝靜脈導管，以便檢查您心臟內血液的容量，並給您開藥。好嗎？

伍德先生： 好的。

護　士： 請把頭轉到右邊，我要用酊劑消毒這個部位，醫生會給您注射局部痲醉藥。可能會覺得有點痛。

伍德先生： 沒關係。

** ———

tincture〔ˈtɪŋktʃɚ〕*n.* 酊劑

anesthetic〔ˌænəsˈθɛtɪk〕*adj.* 痲醉的

✦ Dialogue 2 ✦

Nurse : ***Everything is O. K.***, Mr. Wood. ***You will feel much better soon.*** I'm sorry to disturb you but we will have to insert the catheter to your bladder. This is one of the important procedures and it will make your chest more comfortable.

Mr. Wood : O. K.

** ——————————

bladder〔ˈblædɚ〕*n.*〔解剖〕膀胱

✦ Dialogue 3 ✦

Nurse : How are you feeling?

Mr. Wood : I'm feeling much better now. But why am I so sleepy?

Nurse : Oh, this medicine makes you feel sleepy. We would like to take a chest X-ray soon. But please sleep as much as you can.

✦ 實況會話 2 ✦

護　士： 都很順利，伍德先生。您很快就會覺得舒服多了。很抱歉打擾您，但是我們必須把這根導管插入您的膀胱。這是很重要的手續之一，那會使您的胸部更舒服些。

伍德先生： 好的。

✦ 實況會話 3 ✦

護　士： 您覺得怎麼樣？

伍德先生： 我現在覺得好多了。但是爲什麼會這麼想睡覺呢？

護　士： 噢，這種藥使您覺得想睡覺。雖然我們馬上要做胸部X光檢查。但是請儘量睡吧。

✦ Dialogue 4 ✦

Nurse: The doctor will explain to you about your husband's condition as soon as he finishes his treatment. Mr. Wood is receiving all the treatment he needs, and he is feeling much better now.

Mrs. Wood: Oh, thank you indeed. May I see him?

Nurse: Yes, after you've talked to the doctor. And after that, would you go to the registration desk ***to complete admission procedures with this admission card***?

Mrs. Wood: Certainly. By the way, how long may I stay here?

Nurse: Well, you'll have to ask the doctor.

● 字彙備忘欄 ●

registration office 掛號室
admission procedure 住院手續
catheterization〔 ˌkæθətəraɪˈzeʃən 〕*n.* 導尿法
keep vein opened 保持血管流通
implant of pacemaker 定調植入
congestive heart failure 心臟充血不全
short of breath 呼吸急促

✦ 實況會話 4 ✦

護　士：醫生做完治療後，會馬上向您解釋您先生的情況。伍德先生正在接受所有必須的治療，他現在覺得好多了。

伍德太太：噢，實在很感謝你，我可以看他嗎？

護　士：可以，等您跟醫生談過以後吧。看過您先生以後，請帶著入院許可卡到掛號處，去辦完住院手續，好嗎？

伍德太太：當然好，順便請問我可以在這裡待多久呢？

護　士：唔，您得去問醫生。

《護理重點》

1. 要爲患者打針或治療時，應請陪侍的人到病房外等候。
2. 首先進行必要的治療及檢查，然後要檢視病人的狀況是否穩定，並對家屬詳述醫師的囑咐。
3. 如有 CCU 的會客規定，應加以說明。

護士必背英語句型

1. ***Will you please wait outside the room for a while?***
   ♧ Will you excuse us for a while?
   ♧ Will you please step out for a while?
   請您在房外等一會兒，好嗎？

2. ***I am going to apply some patches on your chest.***
   ♧ I am going to put these patches on your chest.
   ♧ I am going to attach the patches to your chest.
   我要在您的胸部貼一些膠片。

3. ***I am going to clean the area with some tincture.***
   ♧ I am going to sterilize the skin with some tincture.
   ♧ I am going to apply this tincture here.
   我要用一些酊劑來消毒這個部位。

4. ***Everything is O.K.***
   ♧ Everything is going all right.
   ♧ You are doing all right. 事情都很順利。

5. You will feel much better soon, ***because of this medicine.***
   ♧ The medication will soon start to take effect and you will be feeling more comfortable soon.
   因爲藥物的關係，您馬上會覺得舒服多了。

LESSON 20

有關加護病房的指示

Instructions on ICU(Intensive Care Unit)

在加護病房裡，護士向從手術麻醉中甦醒的伍德先生，簡單地説明送他進ＩＣＵ的理由，應儘量不要讓患者有不安的感覺。

並向病人家屬確認醫師的説明。然後對她説明ＩＣＵ的會客時間和方式。

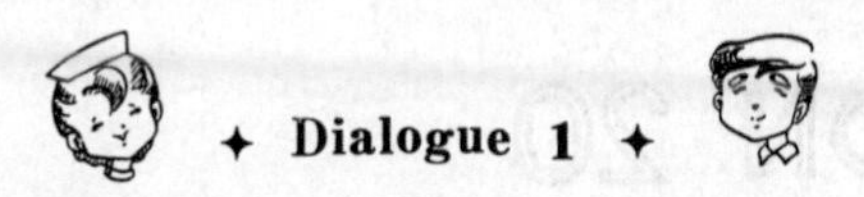

✦ Dialogue 1 ✦

Nurse: Mr. Wood, how are you feeling?

Mr. Wood: O. K.

Nurse: I'm Miss Su. You are in ICU now. ***Your operation was very successful***, but (it) took a little bit longer than expected, so your doctor decided to bring you here where he can observe you more closely.

Mr. Wood: I see

Nurse: This room is not a private room, but we, a health team, stay close to you. ***When you feel that you need your privacy***, you will be able to return to your own room. All right?

Mr. Wood: All right.

** ———

ICU = Intensive Care Unit 加護病房

✦ Dialogue 2 ✦

Nurse: Mrs. Wood.

Mrs. Wood: Yes.

Nurse: Did the doctor explain to you why Mr. Wood is here? And do you have any questions?

Mrs. Wood: He explained to me that ***my husband had a minor irregular heart beat*** during the operation and staying in ICU is much safer for my husband.

✦ 實況會話 1 ✦

護　士：伍德先生，您覺得怎麼樣？

伍德先生：好啊。

護　士：我姓蘇。您現在在加護病房裡。手術非常成功，但是比預計時間要來得久一點，所以醫生決定把您帶來這裡，在這裡他才能更仔細地觀察您。

伍德先生：我知道了。

護　士：這間不是私人病房，而我們醫療小組會緊跟著您，當您覺得需要獨處時，可以回到您自己的病房，好嗎？

伍德先生：好的。

✦ 實況會話 2 ✦

護　士：伍德太太。

伍德太太：是。

護　士：醫生向您解釋過，伍德先生在這裡的原因嗎？您有任何問題嗎？

伍德太太：他向我解釋我先生手術時，有輕微的心律不整，而待在加護病房裡，對我先生會比較安全。

Nurse : All right. In the ICU, your husband has to ***share the room with other patients.*** But we will provide close observation and intensive care for him.

Mrs. Wood : I see.

✦ Dialogue 3 ✦

Nurse : You will be able to see your husband anytime here for 10 minutes every two hours. ***Two people may go in to visit him at one time.*** Please wear an ICU apron.

Mrs. Wood : I see. Is he all right now?

Nurse : Yes, would you like to see him right now?

Mrs. Wood : Yes, I would.

Nurse : He is still half asleep, but don't worry. He will wake up pretty soon.

Mrs. Wood : I see.

Nurse : This way please.

** ───────────

apron〔'eprən〕***n.*** 任何狀似圍裙之物

護　士：對的。在加護病房裡，您先生得和其他病人共用房間。但是我們會給他密切的觀察和集中的看護。

伍德太太：我知道了。

✦ 實況會話 3 ✦

護　士：您可以隨時來這裡看您先生，每次十分鐘，間隔兩小時。可以同時兩個人進去探望他。請穿上加護病房的衣服。

伍德太太：我知道了。他現在好嗎？

護　士：很好，您想立刻去看他嗎？

伍德太太：是的，我想。

護　士：他仍處在半睡眠狀態中，不過用不著擔心，他很快就會醒過來了。

伍德太太：我知道了。

護　士：請這邊走。

•字彙備忘欄•

health team 醫療小組
irregular heart beat 心律不整
minor〔 'maɪnɚ 〕*adj.* 次要的
major〔 'medʒɚ 〕*adj.* 主要的
privacy〔 'praɪvəsɪ 〕*n.* 獨處；隱私
respirator〔 'rɛspə,retɚ 〕*n.* 人工呼吸器
intubation〔 ,ɪntjʊ'beʃən 〕*n.*〔醫〕喉管插入法
pulmonary edema 肺浮腫
dehydration〔 di,haɪ'dreʃən 〕*n.* 脫水
observation〔 ,ɑbzɚ'veʃən 〕*n.* 觀察

《護理重點》

1. 當病患從麻醉中甦醒過來時，護士要以輕鬆的態度，爲病人解釋他爲何進入加護病房，以免其焦慮。如病人情況嚴重，甚至心跳停止，也不可慌張，適當地加以處理，才是要務。並請醫師詳細誠懇地，對其家屬報告狀況，給予他們正確的了解和心理準備。
2. 簡單地說明ICU的會客方式與規定。

護士必背英語句型

1. ***Your operation was very successful.***
   - ♧ Your operation went very well.
   - ♧ Your operation went fine. 您的手術很成功。

2. ***When you feel you need your privacy***, you will be able to return to your own room.
   - ♧ By the time you want your privacy, you will be able to return to your room.

     當您覺得需要獨處時，您可以回到自己的病房。

3. ***My husband had a minor irregular heart beat.***
   - ♧ My husband had a mild irregular heart beat.
   - ♧ My husband is having a slight heart problem.

     我先生有輕微的心律不整。

4. Your husband has to ***share the room with other patients*** in ICU.
   - ♧ There are usually several patients in ICU at the same time. 在加護病房中，您先生得和其他病人共用病房。

5. ***Two people may go in to visit him at one time.***
   - ♧ Two visitors can see him at one time.
   - ♧ He will be able to see two people at one time.

     一次可以有兩個人進去看他。

LESSON 21

對嚴重病患的護理

Reassurance for the Critical Patient

　　對即將死亡、意識狀態漸趨模糊的病患，護士還是儘量減低其對死亡的恐懼。並告訴病人家屬謝絕訪客，以減少病人體力的消耗。

　　伍德先生病情危篤，值夜的護士打電話給病患家屬，同時不忘以和緩關切的語氣，避免給予對方太大的刺激。

　　臨終時，向病人家屬探詢是否需要宗敎上的臨終儀式。

✦ Dialogue 1 ✦

Nurse : George, how are you feeling (now)? I know you are ***breathing very hard. I will stay with you*** as long as possible ***until your family comes*** to see you. Will you open your mouth? I will clean your mouth and give you some water.

✦ Dialogue 2 ✦

Nurse : Mr. Wood seems to be tired by so many visitors. ***Shall we limit the amount of visitors*** to the family and a few friends?

Mrs. Wood : Yes, please, and I will meet the visitors at the front lobby in case ***the visitors are anxious to know his condition.***

✦ 實況會話 1 ✦

護　士：喬治，你（現在）覺得怎麼樣？我知道你呼吸非常困難。我會儘可能陪你久一點，直到你的家人來看你。把嘴巴張開好嗎？我要幫你把嘴巴清理乾淨，並給你一點水。

✦ 實況會話 2 ✦

護　士：伍德先生似乎被那麼多訪客弄累了。要不要限制訪客的人數，只讓家人和一些朋友來呢？

伍德太太：好的，請這麼做吧。如果訪客急著想知道他的病情，我會在前廳接見他們。

✦ Dialogue 3 ✦

Nurse: Hello, is this the Woods' residence?

Mrs. Wood: Yes, it is.

Nurse: This is Miss Su, of ICU, St. Luke's Hospital calling. ***To whom am I speaking***?

Mrs. Wood: This is Mrs. Wood speaking.

Nurse: I'm sorry for calling at this early hour. But your husband's condition has changed. Can you come right away? Do you have anyone else to help you at home?

Mrs. Wood: I am alone. But I'm all right. I will be there soon.

✦ Dialogue 4 ✦

Nurse: ***Are all the family members here*** whom you wanted to notify?

Mrs. Wood: Yes.

Nurse: Sometimes people want their pastor, rabbi, or priest to come. Would you like to call a clergyman?

Mrs. Wood: We are Catholic. Will you please call a Catholic Father right away?

Nurse: Certainly.

✦ Dialogue 3 ✦

護　士：喂，請問是伍德公館嗎？

伍德太太：是的。

護　士：我是聖路克醫院加護病房的蘇小姐，請問您是哪一位?

伍德太太：我是伍德太太。

護　士：抱歉這麼一大早打電話給您，但是您先生的病情發生變化，您能立刻過來嗎？家裡有沒有其他人可以幫您？

伍德太太：我只有一個人，但是不要緊，我會馬上過去。

✦ 實況會話 4 ✦

護　士：您希望通知的家屬全到了嗎？

伍德太太：是的。

護　士：有時候人們會想找他們的新教牧師、猶太教牧師或聖公會牧師來，您想請個牧師來嗎？

伍德太太：我們是天主教徒，你能立刻請一位天主教神父來嗎?

護　士：當然。

●字彙備忘欄●

limit〔'lɪmɪt〕*v*. 限定

pastor〔'pɑstɚ〕*n*. 英國國教以外的新教牧師

rabbi〔'ræbaɪ〕*n*. 猶太教的牧師

clergyman〔'klɝdʒɪmən〕*n*. 牧師

priest〔prist〕*n*. 聖公會的牧師

wheeze〔hwiz〕*v*. 喘息；哮喘

consciousness〔'kɑnʃəsnɪs〕*n*. 知覺

condition〔kən'dɪʃən〕*n*. 情況

cyanotic〔,saɪə'notɪk〕*adj*. 青紫的

suffocate〔'sʌfə,ket〕*v*. 窒息

《護理重點》

1. 在台灣，可能不太習慣直接稱呼病人的名字，但是外國人則認爲直呼名字，特別地親切，使病人較有安全感。
2. 當重病患者的家屬不在時，要避免病人單獨留在病房，應該常去探視或在一旁照顧。
3. 偶爾拉拉患者的手，消除他內心的恐懼不安。
4. 以電話通知病人家屬病況危篤之時，應以緩和的語氣告知，以免給予太大的打擊。
5. 如必須進行臨終宗教儀式，護士應在旁監督，以免妨礙其他患者。

護士必背英語句型

1. You are ***breathing very hard*** now.

   ♧ You are having a hard time breathing now.

   您現在呼吸非常困難。

2. ***I will stay with you until your family comes.***

   ♧ I will sit beside until your family comes.

   ♧ I will be right here with you.

   我會陪您直到您的家人來了爲止。

3. ***Shall we limit the amount of visitors***?

   ♧ Would you like us to set a limit of visitors?

   要不要限制訪客的人數呢？

   ♧ If you would like, we can make an arrangement for you to meet visitors in the lobby.

   如果您要的話，我們可以爲您安排在大廳接見訪客。

4. ***The visitors are anxious to know his condition.***

   ♧ The visitors want to know about your husband's condition.

   ♧ The visitors want to know how he is doing.

   訪客急著想知道他的病情。

5. ***To whom am I speaking***?

   ♧ Who is this speaking, please?

   ♧ Excuse me, but would you please tell me your name?

   請問您是哪一位？（電話用語）

LESSON 22

弔慰

Extending Utmost Sympathy

醫師宣布病人死亡的時候，護士表示由衷的弔慰之情。

家屬和死者告別之後，護士要為死者「淨身」，並探詢家屬有否準備淨身後的「更換衣物」。

會同死者家屬一起清點貴重物品。

醫師在大廳為死者家屬報告病況演變的經過。護士表示哀悼，並慎重地辦理文件及其他手續的安排。

✦ Dialogue 1 ✦

Nurse : Mrs. Wood, ***I really don't know what to say.*** But you have my ***utmost sympathy.***

Mrs. Wood : Oh, Miss Sue, thank you so much. He was such a hard worker and a good man.

Nurse : Yes. I believe so. And you gave all your love to him. Please feel free to stay with him for a while.

✦ Dialogue 2 ✦

Nurse : I would like to ***give your husband a bath.*** After the bath you will be able to see him again. Will you wait for a while in the lobby? Also the doctor would like to talk to you there.

Mrs. Wood : Yes.

Nurse : Excuse me, ***we need your help to check his valuables.***

Mrs. Wood : All right.

Nurse : Do you have any special clothes you want us to put on him?

Mrs. Wood : He has clean pajamas here. ***Will you kindly use these?***

Nurse : Certainly.

✦ 實況會話 1 ✦

護　士：伍德太太，我眞不知道該說什麼才好。但是我向您表示由衷的同情。

伍德太太：噢，蘇小姐，非常感謝你。他是一個這麼勤奮工作的好人。

護　士：是的，我相信是這樣。而您也全心全意地愛他。請別拘束，留下來陪他一會兒。

✦ 實況會話 2 ✦

護　士：我要幫您先生淨身，淨身後，您就可以再看見他了。您到大廳等一會兒好嗎？醫生也想在那裡和您談談。

伍德太太：好的。

護　士：對不起，我們需要您幫忙清點他的貴重物品。

伍德太太：好的。

護　士：您有什麼特別的衣服，要我們幫他穿上嗎？

伍德太太：他在這裡有乾淨的睡衣，請用這些好嗎？

護　士：當然好。

✦ Dialogue 3 ✦

Nurse: Mrs. Wood, have you already ***made any arrangements*** to take the body? If not. ***shall I ask one of the undertakers*** who knows the procedures well?

Mrs. Wood: Yes. Please do so.

Nurse: If you need a certificate, please let us know.

Mrs. Wood: Yes, I will. Thank you.

●字彙備忘欄●

utmost 〔 'ʌt,most 〕 *adj*. 極度的
sympathy 〔 'sɪmpəθɪ 〕 *n*. 同情
pronouncement of death 死亡宣告
expiration 〔 ,ɛkspə'reʃən 〕 *n*. 呼氣；斷氣
document 〔 'dɑkjəmənt 〕 *n*. 文件
postmortem care 善後；死後的處理
certificate 〔 sɚ'tɪfəkɪt 〕 *n*. 證明書
discharge 〔 dɪs'tʃɑrdʒ 〕 *n*. 出院
morgue 〔 mɔrg 〕 *n*. 陳屍間；驗屍處
undertaker 〔 ,ʌndɚ'tekɚ 〕 *n*. 承辦殯葬者；葬儀社
funeral director 葬儀社
autopsy 〔 'ɔtəpsɪ 〕 *n*. 驗屍

✦實況會話 3✦

護　士：伍德太太，您已經安排好怎麼運屍體了嗎？假如沒有，要不要我找一家清楚知道程序的葬儀社呢？

伍德太太：好的，就請這麼辦吧。

護　士：如果您需要死亡證明書，請告訴我們。

伍德太太：好，我會的，謝謝你。

《護理重點》

1. 對病人的死亡應由衷表示哀悼，並且注意不要影響其他病患的情緒。
2. 要仔細觀察病人家屬的心情，不時到病房內探視其家屬，還需要讓他們有充分的時間道別。
3. 應該會同病人家屬一道清點貴重物品，為死亡病患擦洗時，應請其家屬在大廳等候，並詢問是否需要換上特別的宗教服裝。
4. 請醫師說明病況的變化過程，如家屬要求解剖檢查，則應轉告醫師。
5. 從旁指導病人家屬，準備醫院事務及手續上必要的文件，例如領事相關資料等等。

護士必背英語句型

1. I don't know ***what to say.***
   ♧ I really don't know how to express my sorrow.
   我不知道說些什麼才好。

2. ***You have my utmost sympathy.***
   ♧ I am sorry, please accept my deepest sympathy.
   ♧ I would like to extend my heart felt sympathy.
   我向您表示由衷的同情。

3. I would like to ***give your husband a bath.***
   ♧ I would like to take care of your husband's body.
   我要幫您先生淨身。

4. ***We need your help to check his valuables.***
   ♧ We need to go through his valuables, will you help us?
   ♧ We would like you to help us in checking his valuables.
   我們需要您幫忙清點他的貴重物品。

5. ***Will you kindly use these***?
   ♧ Can you please use these?
   ♧ Could you please use these? 請用這些好嗎？

6. Have you already ***made any arrangements*** to take the body?
   ♧ Have you set up any arrangements to take care of the body? 您已經安排好怎麼運屍體了嗎？

7. ***Shall I ask one of the undertakers***?
   ♧ Shall I call on an undertaker for you?
   要不要我找一家葬儀社呢？

LESSON 23

內科的出院指導

Instruction for the Medical Patient

這是護士和即將出院的病患間的談話。首先必須讚美住院病人在恢復健康上所做的努力。還要讓病人了解出院後的護理、飲食治療法、自行注射胰島素的劑量以及保管場所，並確定病人對血糖太低時的急救能力。

✦ Dialogue 1 ✦

Nurse: How are you doing this morning? I would like to give you some information before your discharge.

Mrs. King: Thank you. I am feeling much better.

Nurse: Your blood pressure is stable. Do you know what is the stable blood pressure reading for you?

Mrs. King: Yes. I believe it's about 170 over 98.

Nurse: Yes, that is right. I see that ***you have quit smoking*** already, which is very good for your health.

Mrs. King: Yes, I used to smoke 2 packs a day. Now I almost feel that I don't want to smoke at all.

Nurse: ***That must have been very hard***.

Mrs. King: Yes, it was.

✦ Dialogue 2 ✦

Nurse: Since you have been here, you've been taking 8 gs of salt daily and the dietician has explained to you it is important for you to continue this same amount of salt after you return home.

Mrs. King: I really understand.

Nurse: If ***you develop dizziness***, nausea or headaches, you must call the doctor. Try not to gain weight. Keep doing moderate exercise. This is your card for the outpatient department. Your visit is on the 26th of July.

護　士：您今天早上情況如何？在出院以前，我要提供您一些資料。

金太太：謝謝你，我覺得好多了。

護　士：您的血壓很穩定，您是否知道您穩定的血壓值是多少嗎？

金太太：是的，我認爲是一百七十到九十八左右。

護　士：是的，那就對了。我知道您已經戒煙了，這對健康很有益處。

金太太：是的，我以前一天抽兩包煙，現在我覺得幾乎一點也不想抽煙。

護　士：戒煙的時候一定很難挨。

金太太：是啊。

✦ 實況會話 2 ✦

護　士：自從來這裡以後，您每天攝取八公克的食鹽，營養師也向您解釋過，回家以後繼續攝取同樣份量的食鹽，對您是很重要的。

金太太：我很了解。

護　士：如果您出現頭昏、噁心、或頭痛的現象，一定要打電話給醫生。試著別增加體重，保持適度的運動。這是您的門診卡，七月二十六日要來門診。

Mrs. King : Yes. Thank you.

✦ Dialogue 3 ✦

Nurse : You're going home the day after tomorrow, aren't you?

Mrs. King : Yes.

Nurse : I believe you already know about the kind of diet you should have at home, and also your injection of insulin.

Mrs. King : Yes, and I also have to check my urine with the test tape, don't I?

Nurse : That's right. Do you also know what is the ***normal range of your urine test***?

Mrs. King : Yes, I do.

** ——————————

insulin〔ˈɪnsəlɪn〕*n.* 胰島素

✦ Dialogue 4 ✦

Nurse : Just to make sure, do you know where to keep the insulin?

Mrs. King : Yes, it is in a refrigerator.

Nurse : What amount of insulin do you need at one time?

Mrs. King : I need 0.5 ml which is 20 units, am I right?

Nurse : Yes.

Mrs. King : You know I have already gotten used to it.

金太太：好的，謝謝你。

✦ 實況會話 3 ✦

護　士：您後天要回家，不是嗎？

金太太：是的。

護　士：我相信您已經知道，有關在家裡應該吃的飲食種類，以及胰島素的注射事宜。

金太太：是的，我還得用試紙驗尿，不是嗎？

護　士：對的。您是否也知道您的尿液試驗的正常範圍呢？

金太太：是的，我知道。

✦ 實況會話 4 ✦

護　士：我只想確定一下，您是否知道胰島素要保存在哪裡呢？

金太太：知道，保存在冰箱裡。

護　士：您一次需要多少劑量的胰島素呢？

金太太：我需要 0.5cc，也就是二十單位，對不對？

護　士：對了。

金太太：你是知道的，我已經習慣了。

Nurse : Good. Do you know what kind of symptoms appear if you develop hypoglycemia?

Mrs. King : Yes, cold sweating and some kind of tired feeling like not wanting to do anything.

Nurse : Yes, that is right. If that happens, do you know what to do?

Mrs. King : Yes, I must take sugar at once.

Nurse : You must ***keep sugar or sweets on hand*** all the time.

** ———

hypoglycemia〔,haɪpoglaɪ'simɪə〕*n.*〔醫〕血糖缺乏

symptom〔'sɪmptəm〕*n.* 徵候

●字彙備忘欄●

stable blood pressure reading 穩定的血壓值

used to smoke 有抽煙的習慣

diabetic mellitus 糖尿病

diabetic patient 糖尿病患

angina pectoris 心絞痛；狹心症

myocardial infarction 心肌梗塞

anemia〔ə'nimɪə〕*n.*〔醫〕貧血症

ambulation〔,æmbjə'leʃən〕*n.* 移動；走動

dyspnea〔dɪsp'niə〕*n.*〔醫〕呼吸困難

護　士：很好。您是否知道，如果血糖過低，會出現哪些症狀呢？

金太太：知道，會出冷汗和某種疲勞的感覺，像任何事都不想做之類的。

護　士：是的，那就對了。如果發生那種現象，您知道該怎麼辦嗎？

金太太：知道，我必須馬上吃糖。

護　士：您得隨時把糖或糖果擺在身邊。

**

on hand　在近處；現有

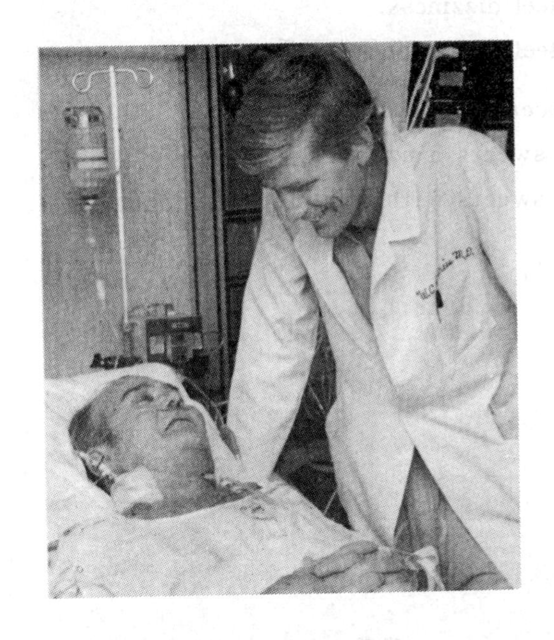

護士必背英語句型

1. ***You have quit smoking.***
   - ♧ You've given up smoking.
   - ♧ You've stopped smoking. 您已經戒煙了。

2. ***That must have been hard.***
   - ♧ You have tried very hard. 您很努力地嘗試。
   - ♧ You have really made up your mind to do it.
     您眞地下決心去做。

3. ***You develop dizziness.***
   - ♧ You feel dizziness.
   - ♧ You feel giddy. 您覺得頭昏。

4. ***Keep sweets on hand.***
   - ♧ Keep sweets handy.
   - ♧ Keep sweets within reach. 把糖果擺在近處。

LESSON 24

開刀手術後的出院指導

Instruction for the Surgical Patient

開刀手術的患者幾天後就可以出院了。護士到病房告訴病人出院後的生活指導，若有任何疑問可以提出，然後開始講解：最好用淋浴不要盆浴，夫妻床事必須在出院後第一次診察時，獲得醫師的許可才行等等。

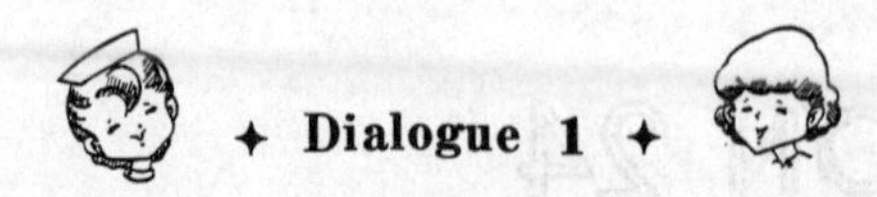

✦ Dialogue 1 ✦

Nurse : ***It is almost time for you to go home.*** So I would like to give you some instructions about what to do after you return home.

Mrs. King : Oh, thank you. Dr. Ma told me that I will be discharged in a few days.

Nurse : If you have any questions as I go through the instructions on how to care for yourself, please stop me.

Mrs. King : All right.

Nurse : First of all, there are no limitations on what you may eat, so please feel free to have anything you wish. Secondly, don't put any pressure or strain on your lower abdomen for another 2 weeks …… ***like lifting heavy objects*** or playing sports, and so on.

Mrs. King : I understand.

** ___

abdomen〔'æbdəmən〕*n.* 下腹

護　士：您差不多該回家了。因此，我想給您一些有關回家以後該怎麼做的指示。

金太太：噢，謝謝你。馬醫師說我在幾天之後出院。

護　士：當我在說明如何照顧您自己時，如果有任何問題，請叫我停下來。

金太太：好的。

護　士：首先，對於您可以吃什麼，並沒有限制，所以，請您隨意地吃您想吃的東西。第二，再下來的兩個禮拜裡，您的下腹部不可以施壓或張力，像提重物或做運動……等等。

金太太：我了解了。

✦ Dialogue 2 ✦

Nurse: In case something occurs, for instance fever, vomiting or abdominal pain, you must call Dr. Ma at the outpatient department during the daytime, or if necessary you may call the emergency room at night.

Mrs. King: Yes, I understand.

Nurse: Of course please feel free to contact us anytime if you have any unusual symptoms or any questions.

Mrs. King: Thank you.

** ———

vomit ['vɑmɪt] *v.* 嘔吐

✦ Dialogue 3 ✦

Nurse: Since you are going home tomorrow, I would like to give you instructions about your life at home.

Mrs. King: Oh, that will be helpful.

Nurse: By the time you leave the hospital, you should have taken a shower and have been out of bed 4 to 6 hours a day. This should be increased gradually by the end of your first week at home. You will probably be living your normal routine, but if you get tired, please do have plenty of rest.

Mrs. King: Yes, I understand.

Nurse: It is best to be up during the day unless you

✦ 實況會話 2 ✦

護　士：如果發生了什麼事，譬如發燒、嘔吐或肚子痛，白天時，您必須打電話到門診部找馬醫師，或者，晚上如果必要的話，您可以打到急診室。

金太太：好的，我懂了。

護　士：如果您有任何不正常的症狀或問題，當然不要拘束，請隨時與我們保持聯絡。

金太太：謝謝您。

✦ 實況會話 3 ✦

護　士：既然您明天要回家了，我想給您一些有關家居生活的指示。

金太太：噢，那對我會很有用。

護　士：您在離開醫院的時候，應該洗過淋浴，並且一天可以下床四至六小時。到您回家的頭一個禮拜終了時，時數應該逐漸增加。您或許會做普通的日常工作，但是如果累了，請務必充分休息。

金太太：好的，我知道。

護　士：白天最好要起來，除非您承當不了或是不舒服。還

don't feel up to it or if ***you feel sick***. Also when you take a shower do not rub your incision and a tub bath should not be taken unless told otherwise to do so by your doctor.

Mrs. King : Yes.

** ———————————

feel up to 以為承當得了；以為吃得消

✦ Dialogue 4 ✦

Nurse : One more thing, please do not have sexual relationships until the doctor tells you that it is all right.

Mrs. King : May I ask the doctor about that?

Nurse : Surely, ***do not hesitate to ask him***. He will be happy to answer any questions you may have.

Mrs. King : O.K.

Nurse : Please feel free to call the duty doctor here at the hospital anytime if you have a sudden severe lower abdominal pain, chill, fever, bleeding from the vagina more than a menstrual period and pain or burning sensation when you urinate.

Mrs. King : Oh, that is good to know. Thank you.

** ———————————

vagina 〔vəˈdʒaɪnə〕 *n.* 〔解剖〕陰道

有當您淋浴時，不要擦到切口，您應該不要洗盆浴，除非醫生另外告訴您要洗盆浴。

金太太：好的。

✦ 實況會話 4 ✦

護　士：還有一件事，請不要發生性關係，直到醫生告訴您那樣沒事才可以。

金太太：我可以問醫生有關那方面的事嗎？

護　士：當然可以，別猶豫儘管問他。他會很樂意回答您可能有的任何問題。

金太太：好的。

護　士：如果您突然下腹劇痛、發冷、發熱、經期以外的陰道出血、小便時有疼痛或灼熱的感覺，請不要客氣，隨時打電話到醫院，給值班醫師。

金太太：噢，聽到這眞好。謝謝你。

** ───────────────

menstrual〔ˈmɛnstrʊəl〕*adj.* 月經的

護士必背英語句型

1. ***It is almost time for you to go home.***
   - ♧ You are ready to go home.
   - ♧ You are going home pretty soon. 您差不多快回家了。
2. ***… like lifting heavy objects***
   - ♧ like carrying heavy things
   - ♧ like pushing up big objects 像提重物之類
3. ***You feel sick.***
   - ♧ You feel ill.
   - ♧ You feel weak. 您不舒服。
4. ***Do not hesitate to ask.***
   - ♧ Don't be reluctant to ask.
   - ♧ Don't hold back to speak up. 別猶豫儘管問。

●字彙備忘欄●

unusual symptom 異常症狀
incision〔ɪn'sɪʒən〕*n.* 切口
sexual relationship 性關係
no limitation 沒有限制
woman's disease 婦女病
time for ovulation 排卵期
external genitalia 外陰部
unpleasant odor 臭味
intrauterine〔,ɪntrə'jutərɪn〕*adj.* 子宮內的
contraceptive medicine 避孕藥

LESSON 25

小兒科和婦產科的出院指導

Instruction for the New-Mother and the Pediatric Patient

凱瑟琳的出院指導是由她的母親代理的。做母親的很擔心，護士儘量具體地為她解說皮膚的護理，減少她的憂慮。並將複診預約單，填好日期交給她。

護士再走到產後要和小孩一起出院的母親病房中，對她說明子宮復元的相關事項，以及出院後，排完尿仍要做會陰部的清洗。

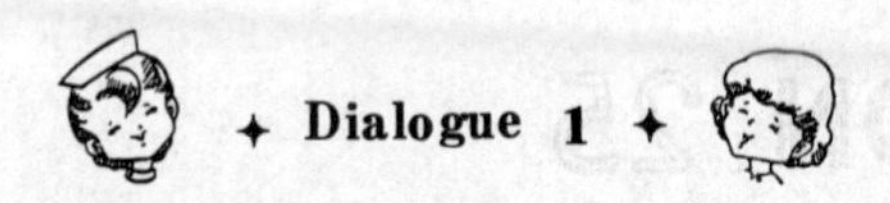

✦ Dialogue 1 ✦

Nurse : Hello. How are you?

Mother : Fine, thank you.

Nurse : I would like to tell you about ***how to care for Catherine*** following her discharge.

Mother : Thank you.

Nurse : As you know, Catherine will ***need to have check-ups***.

Mother : Yes, when will we get her appointment card?

Nurse : This is your card for next week, it's on the 26th of July from 9 to 10 o'clock. Please don't lose this card.

Mother : Thank you, but ***I am afraid to take her home.***

Nurse : I understand, but she is ready, and you know you can call us anytime you wish.

Mother : Yes, I know.

✦ Dialogue 2 ✦

Nurse : At home she may take a tub bath but not for a long time, because she may get tired. Please do not try to peel her skin. If it is forced off, it might get infected.

Mother : You mean I should just leave it alone?

Nurse : Yes, as it dries, it will gradually come off by itself.

Mother : I see.

✦ 實況會話 1 ✦

護　士：嗨，您好嗎？

母　親：很好，謝謝。

護　士：我要告訴您，關於凱瑟琳出院後，如何照顧她的事情。

母　親：謝謝。

護　士：正如您所知道的，凱瑟琳得做健康檢查。

母　親：是的，我們什麼時候可以拿到她的預約卡呢？

護　士：這是下禮拜的卡，是七月二十六日，從九點到十點，請不要把這張卡遺失了。

母　親：謝謝你，但我怕帶她回家。

護　士：我了解。但是她已經好多了，而且您知道，您隨時可以打電話給我們。

母　親：是的，我知道。

✦ 實況會話 2 ✦

護　士：在家裡，她可以洗盆浴，但不能太久，因爲她會累。請不要試著替她剝皮，如果皮膚用力剝落的話，可能會受到感染。

母　親：你是說，我應該不去理它嗎？

護　士：是的，當它乾了以後，它自己會逐漸脫落的。

母　親：我懂了。

Nurse: Do you have anything to ask?

Mother: Yes, it seems to me that her skin has become very dry. Doesn't it need to have any oil or lotion?

Nurse: No, because some parts are still red. Can you see here? See, which means it isn't quite healed yet. However this reddish skin will soon become dry, and it will peel off spontaneously.

Mother: Oh, I understand. ***Will it get itchy when it peels?***

Nurse: Perhaps a little, but not much. If necessary, the doctor will give you some oil for her skin.

Mother: Thank you.

Nurse: The doctor will tell you when she is able to go to kindergarten. It will probably take another 2 to 3 weeks. But, of course, she may play with her toys and also take a walk every day, but have her take a rest in the afternoon. If she looks pale, weak or vomits and loses her appetite, please call her doctor.

**

infect〔ɪn'fɛkt〕*v.* 傳染

itchy〔'ɪtʃɪ〕*adj.* 癢的

護　士：您還要問什麼嗎？

母　親：是的，我覺得她的皮膚似乎變得很乾燥。難道不需要抹些油或乳液嗎？

護　士：不用，因爲有些部位還紅紅的。您看到了嗎？看，這就表示還未痊癒。然而這層紅色的皮膚，很快就會變乾，而且會自然脫落。

母　親：噢，我懂了。當它脫落時，會不會癢？

護　士：也許有一點癢，但不會很癢。如果需要的話，醫生會給您一些油來抹她的皮膚。

母　親：謝謝您。

護　士：醫生會告訴您，她什麼時候能上幼稚園。或許得再過兩、三個禮拜。但是，她當然可以每天玩玩具，也可以散步，不過下午要讓她休息。如果她看起來蒼白、虛弱，或是嘔吐，沒有食慾，請打電話給她的醫生。

** ___

spontaneously〔spɑnˈtenɪəslɪ〕*adv.* 自然地；自發地

vomit〔ˈvɑmɪt〕*v.* 嘔吐

✦ Dialogue 3 ✦

Nurse : Tomorrow you are going home with your baby, aren't you?

Mrs. King : Yes, and ***I am excited.***

Nurse : I would like to give you some instructions about what you may and may not do at home.

Mrs. King : All right.

Nurse : The uterus returns to its previous position in 4 to 6 weeks time after childbirth. The vaginal discharge continues for 4 to 6 weeks also. So long as there is discharge, it is necessary to care for yourself after urination in the same way as you have been doing now.

Mrs. King : I see.

** ———

uterus〔'jutərəs〕*n.* 子宮

●字彙備忘欄●

appointment card 預約卡
check up 檢查
peel〔pil〕*v.* 剝落
previous〔'priviəs〕*adj.* 先前的
sweat gland 汗腺
petechia〔pə'tɛkiə〕*n.*〔醫〕瘀點；瘀斑
blister〔'blɪstɚ〕*n.* 膿疱、水泡
tumor〔'tjumɚ〕*n.*〔醫〕腫瘤

✦ 實況會話 3 ✦

護　士：明天您要和您的寶寶回家了，不是嗎？

金太太：是的，我很興奮。

護　士：我想給您一些有關在家裡什麼可以做什麼不可以做的指示。

金太太：好的。

護　士：生產後四到六個星期以後，子宮會回復到它以前的位置。陰道分泌物也持續四到六個星期。只要有分泌物，排尿後您就必須照現在做的同樣方法來處理。

金太太：知道了。

** ──────────

discharge〔dɪsˈtʃardʒ〕*n.* 分泌物

●字彙備忘欄●

erosion〔ɪˈroʒən〕*n.*〔醫〕糜爛
dermatitis〔ˌdɝməˈtaɪtɪs〕*n.* 皮膚炎
ointment〔ˈɔɪntmənt〕*n.* 軟膏
eczema〔ˈɛksɪmə〕*n.*〔醫〕濕疹
scratch〔skrætʃ〕*v.* 抓、搔
dermatology〔ˌdɝməˈtɑlədʒɪ〕*n.* 皮膚科
rash〔ræʃ〕*n.* 發疹
pimple〔ˈpɪmpl̩〕*n.* 粉刺、面皰

護士必背英語句型

1. ***how to care for Catherine***
   - ♧ how to take care of Catherine
   - ♧ how to look after Catherine 如何照顧凱塞琳

2. ***She needs to have checkups.***
   - ♧ She needs to have follow-up visits.
   - ♧ She still needs to be under the care of a doctor.
     她需要檢查治療。

3. ***I am afraid to take her home.*** 我怕帶她回家。
   - ♧ I am worried about how to take care of her at home.
   - ♧ I am anxious about taking care of her at home.
     我很擔心在家裡怎麼照顧她。

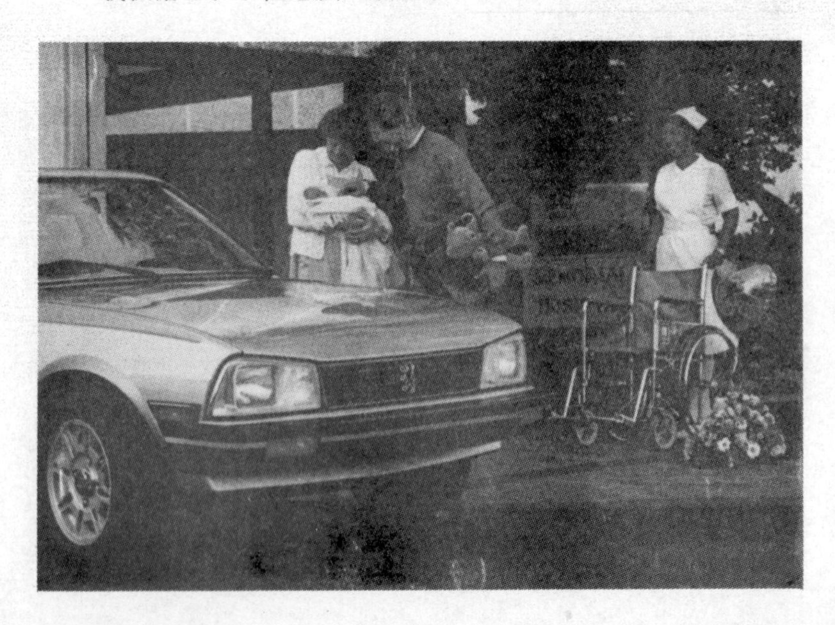

LESSON 26

住院、出院、轉病房的手續

Procedure of Admission, Transfer and Discharge

病人來辦理住院手續。由於外國都付有保險金，所以支付方法不太一樣。護士向她說明住院時必須先付現款，數週之後可以領回退費，然後由專人帶領到病房。

由於患者希望住個人單獨的房間，所以替他轉了病房，並說明不同的收費情形。獲准出院時，告知病人付清醫藥費，即可搬回家去。

✦ Dialogue 1 ✦

Mrs. King : I need to be admitted.

Nurse : I see. Will you please ***fill in these forms***? Please use this counter to fill them in. I will help you.

Mrs. King : Thank you.

Nurse : What kind of insurance do you have?

Mrs. King : I have Blue Cross and Blue Shield.

Nurse : All right. When we receive these forms from you, we will fill them in and if you would like, we will send them directly to the company.

Mrs. King : I see.

** ______________________

Blue Cross 美國的一個非營利性會員組織，代會員繳付若干醫藥費用

✦ Dialogue 2 ✦

Nurse : I would like to make sure you know that you will have to pay the full amount in cash when you are discharged. But ***you will be reimbursed*** by your insurance company.

Mrs. King : I see, then how long does it usually take?

Nurse : It usually takes a few weeks. Because we can't fill out the forms until the treatments are all completed. But we will do our best to have it done as quickly as possible.

Mrs. King : All right, but nurse, I don't have a seal.

金太太： 我要辦住院。

護　士： 我知道了。請填寫這些表格好嗎？請在這個櫃台填寫，我會幫您的。

金太太： 謝謝你。

護　士： 您有哪一種保險呢？

金太太： 我有藍十字和藍盾的保險。

護　士： 好的。當我們收到您的這些表格時，會把它們填進去。如果您要的話，我們會把他們直接寄到保險公司去。

金太太： 知道了。

** ――――――――――

Blue Shield 美國的醫藥保險之一，投保人住院才付費，平常生病不管。

✦ 實況會話 2 ✦

護　士： 我想確定一下，您是否知道出院的時候，全部費用必須用現金付款呢？但是您的保險公司會退款給您。

金太太： 我知道了，那麼通常要多久呢？

護　士： 通常要好幾個禮拜。因爲我們要等醫療全部結束，才能填好表格。但是，我們會盡全力快點辦好這件事。

金太太： 好的，但是護士小姐，我沒有印章。

Nurse : You can just sign it. When you have filled in your forms, please let me know and I will take you to your floor.

✦ Dialogue 3 ✦

Nurse : We have a private room available now. ***Would you like to transfer to it***?

Mrs. King : Yes, very much. When will that be possible?

Nurse : This afternoon, Miss Ku will come and ***help you gather your things***.

Mrs. King : Yes.

Nurse : Do you know the price difference?

Mrs. King : No, I am not quite sure.

Nurse : I see, then I will call to the admitting office and someone from there will explain the various room charges to you. Oh, would you like to see the room before you move there?

Mrs. King : Yes, I would like to.

Nurse : Do you like it?

Mrs. King : Yes, I do.

Nurse : You are going home today. It has been 10 days, hasn't it?

Mrs. King : Yes, what time may I go home?

Nurse : Any time after you have paid your hospital bill.

Mrs. King : Do I have to take some particular papers to the accounting office?

Nurse : No, we have sent the necessary forms already, so

護　士：您只要簽名就行了。當您填好表格以後，請告訴我，
我會帶您到那一層樓去。

✦ 實況會話 3 ✦

護　士：我們現在空出一間單人房，您想搬進去嗎？

金太太：好的，我很想搬。什麼時候可以搬呢？
護　士：今天下午，顧小姐會來幫您收拾東西。

金太太：好的。
護　士：您知道價錢的差別嗎？
金太太：不，我不太清楚。
護　士：哦，那麼我會打電話到住院室，那裡會有人來向您
解釋不同病房的收費。噢，在您搬到那裡以前，您
想先看看房間嗎？

金太太：好的，我想看看。
護　士：您喜歡嗎？
金太太：是的，我喜歡。

護　士：您今天要回家了，已經十天了，不是嗎？

金太太：是啊，我幾點可以回去呢？
護　士：在您付了住院費以後，隨時都可以。
金太太：我必須帶些特別的文件去會計室嗎？

護　士：不用，我們已經把必須的表格送過去了，所以您只

just go down to the accounting office. I think you know where it is, on the first floor. This is your appointment card for Dr. Ma. It's for the 26th of July between 9 and 10 o'clock.

Mrs. King : Thank you.

● 字彙備忘欄 ●

insurance〔ɪn'ʃʊrəns〕*n*. 保險
fill in 塡好
reimburse〔,riɪm'bɝs〕*v*. 退款
private room 單人病房
transfer〔træns'fɝ〕*v*. 遷移
semi-private room 半單人病房（也可當雙人房）
form〔fɔrm〕*n*. 表格
hospital bill 住院費
accounting office 會計室
two bed room 雙人病房
ward/general room 大病房
front lobby 前廳
gift shop 禮品店
pharmacy〔'fɑrməsɪ〕*n*. 藥房
ambulance〔'æmbjələns〕*n*. 救護車

要到下面的會計室就行了。我想您知道在哪裡，在一樓。這是您和馬醫師的預約卡，時間是七月二十六日，九點到十點之間。

金太太： 謝謝您。

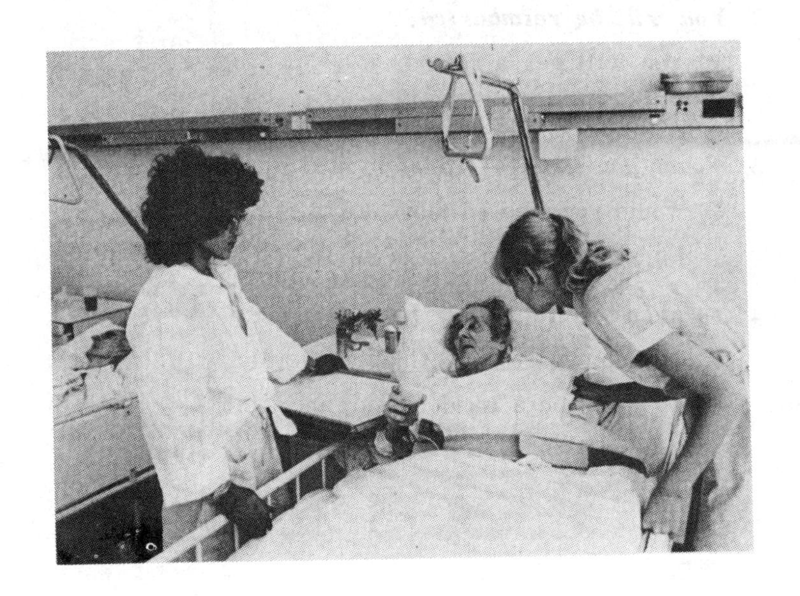

護士必背英語句型

1. ***Fill in these forms.***
   - ♧ Fill out these forms.
   - ♧ Complete these forms. 填寫這些表格。

2. ***You will be reimbursed.***
   - ♧ You will get a refund.
   - ♧ You will get your money back. 錢會退還給您。

3. ***Would you like to transfer to it?***
   - ♧ Would you like to move in to it?
   - ♧ Do you want to change to it? 您想搬進去嗎?

4. ***to help you to gather your things***
   - ♧ to help you to put things together
   - ♧ to give you a hand to tidy up a bit 幫您收拾東西

附　　錄

1 醫護專門術語

◑ 醫 師

Attending doctor (*physician*) 主治醫師

Duty doctor (*doctor on call*) 值班醫師

Home doctor (*family doctor*) 家庭醫師

Resident doctor 住院醫師

◑ 科名及專科醫師

Internal medicine 內科

Internist 內科醫師

Surgery 外科

Surgeon 外科醫師

Pediatrics 小兒科

Pediatrician 小兒科醫師

Gynecology 婦科(醫學)

Gynecologist 婦科醫師

Obstetrics 產科

Obstetrician 產科醫師

Orthopedics 整形外科

Orthopedist 整形外科醫師

Urology 泌尿科

Urologist 泌尿科醫師

Psychiatry 精神科

Psychiatrist 精神科醫師

Neurology 神經科

Neurologist 神經科醫師

◑ 病 歷

Clinical history 病歷

History of present illness 現病病歷

Family history 家族病歷

◑ 不舒服的症狀

Hiccups　呃逆；打嗝

Belching, Burping　噯氣

Running nose　流鼻水　　**Gurgling**　咕嚕聲；腹鳴

Cold sweating　冷汗　　**Diaphoresis**　發汗；出汗

◑ 疼痛的種類

Burning pain　灼痛　　**Dull pain**　鈍痛

Throbbing pain　搏動痛；抽痛

Sharp pain　銳痛；急痛

Splitting pain　劇痛　　**Stabbing pain**　刺痛

Colic pain　腹部絞痛；疝痛

Sore　粘膜或糜爛的疼痛

(*Sore throat*, *Sore skin*)（喉嚨痛、皮膚痛）

Hurt　來自外部的疼痛　(*This needle hurts.*)

Ache　身體的部分疼痛（接於身體的部分之後）

(*Toothache*, *Headache*)（牙痛、頭痛）

◑ 症　狀

Orthopnea　直體呼吸；端坐呼吸

Nasal breathing　鼻呼吸

Deep breathing　深呼吸　　**Fainting**　昏倒

Irritated, Restless　躁動；不安

Tension　緊張　　**Tachypnea**　呼吸迫促

Bradypnea　呼吸徐緩　　**Apnea**　窒息

Tachycardia　心搏過速

Bradycardia　心跳徐緩（通常每分鐘少於 60 次）

Spasm, Cramp, Convulsion　痙攣

Tonic spasm　强直性痙攣

Clonic spasm　間歇性痙攣

Grand mal　癲癎大發作

Petit mal　癲癎小發作

◑ 分泌物

Gastric juice　胃液　　Sputum　咯痰；唾液

Character　特徵

◑ 體　位

Position change　體位交換　　Restrain　抑制

Supine position　仰臥位　　Side position　側臥位

Sitting position　起坐位　　Prone position　俯臥位

Knee-chest position　膝胸位

Lithotomy position　截石位；截石術臥位

◑ 藥　品 medication

⇨按服用方式區分的藥品

Oral medicine　口服藥

Hypodermic injection　皮下注射

Intramuscular injection　肌肉注射

Intravenous injection　靜脈內注射

Intravenous drip injection　靜脈點滴注射

Epidural injection　硬膜外注射

External medicine　外用藥

Rectal suppository　直腸坐藥

Vaginal suppository　膣坐藥

⇨按用途區分的藥品

Laxative 輕瀉藥　**Digestant** 消化劑
Antibiotics 抗生素　**Diuretics** 利尿劑

◑ 麻　醉 anesthesia

General anesthesia 全身麻醉　**Local anesthesia** 局部麻醉
Spinal anesthesia 脊椎麻醉
Epidural anesthesia 硬膜外麻醉

◑ 醫療器材

Thermometer 溫度計；檢溫器　**Stethoscope** 聽診器
Blood pressure apparatus 血壓計
Commode 坐椅式便器　**Urinal** 尿壺
Bed pan 便器　**Kidney basin** 膿盆
Forceps 鉗子；鑷子　**Scissors** 剪刀
Sound 探子；探條　**Tongue depressor** 壓舌板；壓舌器
Stretcher 擔架；輸送車　**Wheelchair** 輪椅
Dressing cart 敷料車　**Cart** 手推車
Rubber sheet 橡皮單　**Blanket** 毛毯
Gown 睡衣　**Underwear** 內衣
Bedcradle, cage 護架　**Ring-stand** 環支架
Icebag 冰袋　**Compress** 壓布；罨布
Ice pillow 冰枕　**Bedside table** 床頭桌

◑ 其　他

Complication 併發症　**Indication** 指徵；適應徵
Prescription 處方；藥方

2 常用醫護縮寫字

—A—

aa of each 對每一個；各

abd abdomen 腹部

ac before meals 飯前

ACC *or* **AnCC** anodal closure contraction 陽極閉時收縮

ad to add 添加

ad lib as desired 任意；隨意

adm admission 住院

AFB acid-fast bacillus 抗酸桿菌

alt hor alternis horis 每隔一小時

a.m. morning 上午

amt amount 量

anes anesthesia 痲醉

A-P-L anterior-pituitary-like substance 垂體前葉樣物質

aq water 水

ASA aspirin 阿斯匹靈

ASHD arteriosclerotic heart disease 動脈硬化心臟病

ax axillary 腋窩

—B—

B boron or bacillus 硼；桿菌

Ba Barium 鋇

BCG Bacillus Calmette et Guerin 卡介菌

Be berryllium 鈹

b i d twice daily 每日兩次

BM bowel movement 腸蠕動

BMR basal metabolism rate 基礎代謝速率

BNA Basle Nomina Anatomica 巴賽爾解剖

BP blood pressure 血壓

BPH benign prostatic hypertrophy 良性前列腺肥大

BRP bathroom privileges 浴室特權

BSP Bromosulfophthalein 溴酚酚磺酸

BUN blood urea nitrogen 血尿素氮質

—C—

C centrigrade 十進位

c with 用、偕、與

Ca (1) calcium,(2) cancer (1)鈣，(2)癌

CaCC cathodal closure contraction 陰極閉時收縮

cal small calory 小卡

Cal large calory 大卡

C&S culture and sensitivity 培養及敏感性

cap(s) capsule(s) 膠囊
CBC complete blood count 全血計量
cc cubic centimeter 立方公分
CC chief complaint 主訴
Cel Celsius 攝氏溫度
C.H.F. congestive heart failure 充血性心臟衰竭
cl chlorine 氯
cm centimeter 公分
CNS central nervous system 中樞神經系統
CO_2 carbon dioxide 二氧化碳
CS central supply dept. 供應中心
CSF cerebrospinal fluid 大腦脊髓
CTDB cough, turn, deep-breathe 咳嗽、頭暈、深呼吸
CV cardiovascular 心臟血管的
CVA (1) cerebral vascular accident, (2) costal vertebral angle (1)腦中風，(2)肋骨椎骨角
cysto cystoscopy 膀胱鏡檢法

—D—

D&C dilation and curettage 擴張術及刮除術
D/C(DC) discontinue 中止
def defecate 澄清，排除
dept department 部門
diff differentiation 鑑別，分化
dil dilute 稀釋的
DOA dead on arrival 出生或到達時死亡
DOE dyspnea on exertion 用力時呼吸困難
D.R. reaction of degeneration 變性反應；變質反應
dr drachm(s) 英錢(約等於四公分)
D_5S dextrose (glucose) in saline 生理食鹽水中加入5%的葡萄糖
DSD dry sterile dressing 乾的無菌敷料
dsg dressing 敷料
D_5W 5% dextrose (glucose) in water 水中加入5%的葡萄糖
Dx diagnosis 診斷

—E—

ECG electrocardiogram 心電圖
EEG electroencephalogram 腦電波
EENT eye, ear, nose, and throat 眼、耳、鼻、喉
EKG electrocardiogram 心電圖
elix elixir 特效藥
ENT ear, nose, throat 耳、鼻、喉
ESR erythrocyte sedimentation rate 紅血球沉降速率
exc excision 切除
exp lap exploratory laparotomy 探測性剖腹術
ext extract 萃取

—F—

F Fahrenheit 華氏溫度計
FBS fasting blood suger 飢餓血糖值
Fe iron 鐵

$FeSO_4$ ferrous sulfate 硫酸亞鐵
FH family history 家族史
fl fluid 液；液體
fl. dr. fluid dram 量錢
fl. oz. fluid ounce 量嘔；液嘔
fol leaves 葉
ft foot, let there be made 呎；製成
ft. mas. fiat massa 製爲塊劑
ft. mist. fiat mistura 製爲合劑
ft. pl. fiat pilula 製爲丸劑
ft. pulv. fiat pulvis 製爲散劑
FUO fever of undetermined origin 原因未明的發燒
fx fracture 骨折

—G—

g *or* **gm** gram 公克
GB gallbladder 膽囊
Gc gonococcus 淋球菌
GI gastrointestinal 胃腸
gr grain 喱
GTT glucose tolerance test 葡萄糖耐量測試
gtt(s) drop(s) 滴
GU genitourinary 生殖；泌尿的
Gyn gynecology 婦科學

—H—

h hour 小時
Hb *or* **Hgb** hemoglobin 血紅素；紅血球素
Hcl hydrocholoric acid 鹽酸
hct hematocrit 血比容
h.d. at bedtime 睡時（服藥）
HCVD hypertensive cardiovascular disease 高血壓性心臟血管疾病
Hg mercury 汞
HNP herniated nucleus pulposus 脊柱髓核凸出
HNV has not voided 未排出
HO house office 診療室
H_2O water 水
H_2O_2 hydrogen peroxide 雙氧水
hor. decub. at bedtime 臨睡（服）
H & P history and physical 過去病史和身體檢查
hs at bedtime (hour of sleep) 睡前（服）
Ht total hyperopia 完全遠視

—I—

ia if awake 如果醒過來
Id one's own 染色粒
I & D incision and drainage 切開並引流
I & O intake and output 輸入量與輸出量
IM intramuscular 肌肉內
inc incontinent 失禁
I-para primipara 初產婦
IPPB intermittent positive pressure breathing 間歇性陽壓呼吸
I.Q. intelligence quotient 智力商
IU international unit 國際單位
IV intravenous 靜脈內

IVP intravenous pyelogram 靜脈內腎盂攝影術

—J—

J Joule's equivalent 焦耳氏當量

—K—

K potassium 鉀
Ka kathode or cathode 陰極
KCC kathodal closing contraction 陰極閉時收縮
KCI potassium chloride 氯化鉀
kg kilogram 仟克，公斤
KOC kathodal opening contraction 陰極開時收縮
KST kathodal closing tetanus 陰極閉時強直
K.V. kilovolt 千伏特
K.W. kilowatt 千瓦德
KUB kidney ureter bladder 腎臟、尿道、膀胱

—L—

L liter 升
lab laboratory 實驗室
lb *or* **lib** pound 磅
lg large 大
liq liquid 液體
LLL left lower lobe 左下葉
LLQ left lower quadrant 左下四分之一
LMD local medical doctor 開業醫生
LMP, *or* **LNMP** (on female chart) last (normal) menstrual period (女性病歷表)上一次月經的最後一天
loc. dol to the painful place 用於痛處
LP lumbar puncture 腰椎穿刺
LUL left upper lobe 左上葉
LUQ left upper quadrant 左上四分之一

—M—

M thousand, mix, muscle 千、合劑、肌肉
m minim, meter 量滴、公尺
ma milliampere 毫安培
mac to macerate 浸軟
M.E.D. minimal erythema dose 最小紅斑量
mEq millequivalent 毫克當量
Mf Microfilaria 幼絲蟲
m.f.d. microfarad 法拉(百萬分之一法拉)
mg milligram 毫克，公絲
$MgSO_4$ magnesium sulfate 硫酸鎂
MI myocardial infarction 心肌梗塞
min minim; minute 量滴；分鐘
ml milliliter 毫升
M.L.D. minium lethal dose 最小致死量
mm millimeter 公厘
mod moderate 中等量
MOM milk of magnesia 鎂乳液

M.U. Maché unit; mouse unit 馬歇單位；小鼠單位

μg microgram 百萬分之一克

——N——

n nerve 神經

Na sodium 鈉

NaCl sodium chloride 氯化鈉

NG(N/G) nasogastric 鼻胃

N.N.R. New and Nonofficial Remedies 成藥集

no number 數目

noc night 夜間

NPN nonprotein nitrogen 非蛋白氮質，餘氮

NPO nothing by mouth 禁食

NS normal saline 生理食鹽水

NTG nitroglycerin 硝化甘油

N.Y.D. not yet diagnosed 尚未診定

——O——

O & P ova and parasites 寄生蟲及卵

OB obstetrics 產科學

O.D. right eye 右眼

od once daily 每天一次

O.L. left eye 左眼

on once nightly 每晚一次

OOB out of bed 離床

op operation 手術

OPD outpatient department 門診部

OR operating room 手術室

OS left eye 左眼

os mouth 口

OT (1) old tuberculin, (2) occupational therapy (1)舊結核菌素，(2)職能療法

O_2 oxygen 氧

OU both eyes 兩眼

oz ounce 盎司盎

——P——

P (1) pulse, (2) phosphorus (1)脈博，(2)磷

P_2 pulmonic second sound 肺動脈第二音

$\bar{P}$ after 之後

PABA para-aminobenzoic acid 對氨安息香酸

PBI protein-bound iodine 蛋白質結合碘

p.c. after meals 飯後

PE physical examination 身體檢查

per by 每

PERLA pupils equal, react to light, accommodate 瞳孔對稱，對光有反應，兩眼協調

pH hydrogen-ion concentration 氫離子濃度

PI present illness 現在病況

PM post mortem 死後

p.m. afternoon 下午

PO predominating organisms 主要的生物

po by mouth 口服

post-op after operation 手術後

pre-op before operation 手術前

prn whenever necessary 需要時

PSP phenolsulphonphtahlein test 酚磺酞試驗

PT physiotherapy 物理療法

pt pint 品脫

PTA prior to admission 入院前

pulv to powder 粉末狀

P.U.O. pyrexia of unknown origin 戰壕熱

—Q—

q.d. four times daily 每天四次

q.h. every hour 每小時

q.i.d. four times a day 每天四次

q.l. as much as is desired 隨意量

q.n. every night 每晚

q.o.d. every other day 每隔一天

q.p. at will 隨意量

q.q.h. every fourth hour 每逢四小時

q.s. quantity sufficient 足量

qt quart 夸爾

q_2h every two hours 每兩個小時

q.v. as much as you like; which see 隨意量；參閱

—R—

R (1) rectal, (2) respiration, (3) right, (4) rough colony (1)直腸，(2)呼吸，(3)右，(4)粗糙菌集落

Rad. root 根

RAI radioactive isotope 放射性同位素

RBC red blood cells (*or* count) 紅血球

Reg regular (diet) 普通(飲食)

RLL right lower lobe 右下葉

RLQ right lower quadrant 右下四分之一

RIO rule out 考慮排除；懷疑；疑似

ROS review of systems 系統檢查

RUL right upper lobe 右上葉

RUQ right upper quadrant 右上四分之一

Rx (1) prescribed, (2) treated (1)處方，(2)治療

—S—

$\bar{s}$ without 沒有

sat saturate 飽和

sc subcutaneous 皮下

sed rate sedimentation rate 沉降速率

SG specific gravity 比重

sig to write 簽名

sm small 小

SOB short of breath 呼吸短促

sol solution 溶液

SOS if necessary (one does) 需要的話給與一次

SP suprapubic 恥骨上方

spec specimen 檢體

sp gr specific gravity 比重

SPP suprapubic prostatectomy 恥骨上方前列腺切除術

SS soap solution 肥皂溶液

$\bar{ss}$ one-self 一半

SSE soapsuds enema 肥皂凍灌腸

Staph Staphylococcus 葡萄球菌

stat immediately 立刻

Strep Streptococcus 鏈球菌

STS serological test for syphillis 梅毒血清學測驗

Sx symptom 症狀

—T—

T (1) temperature, (2) tablespoon (1)溫度，(2)大茶匙

t teaspoon 小茶匙

TB tuberculosis 結核病

tbc tuberculosis 結核病

tbsp tablespoon 大茶匙

tid three times a day 一天三次

tinct tincture 奎寧藥

TLC tender loving care 溫柔富愛心的照顧

TP total protein 全蛋白質

TPR temperature, pulse, respiration 體溫、脈博、呼吸

trach tracheostomy 氣管切開術

tsp teaspoon 小茶匙

TV tidal volume 肺活量

TWE tap water enema 自來水灌腸

—U, V, W—

U unit 單位

UCHD usual childhood disease 小兒科常見疾病

ung ointment 軟膏

URI upper respiratory infection 上呼吸道感染

VD venereal disease 性病

via by way of 經由

VS vital signs 生命徵象

Wass Wasserman 瓦氏梅毒血清檢驗法

WBC white blood cell (count) 白血球（或計數）

WNWD well nourished, well developed 營養良好，發育良好

wt weight 體重

3 醫護字根字首須知

與身體器官有關的字首

aden-	gland	腺體
angi-	vessel	管
aniso-	unequal	不等
arthr-	joint	關節
aur-	ear	耳朵
blephar(o)-	eyelid	眼瞼
cardi-	heart	心臟
cephal-	head	頭
cerebr-	brain	腦
cervic-	neck	頸
cheili-	lip	唇
chol-	bile	膽汁
cost-	rib	肋骨
crani-	skull	頭顱
cut-	skin	皮膚
cyst-	bladder	囊
cyt-	cell	細胞
dent-	tooth	牙齒
dermato-	skin	皮膚
encephal-	brain	腦
enter-	intestine	腸
episio-	pubes	會陰；陰部
gastro-	stomach; belly	胃；腹
genito-	genital	生殖器
gingiv-	gums	齒齦
gloss-	tongue	舌
hem(o)-	blood	血液
hepat-	liver	肝臟
hyster-	uterus	子宮
irido-	iris	虹膜
laparo-	loin, abdomen	腹
laryng-	windpipe	氣管
lip-	fat	脂肪
lith-	stone	石頭
mamm-	breast	乳房
mast-	breast	乳房
mening-	membrane	粘膜
musculo-	muscle	肌
my-	muscle	肌肉
myel-	bone marrow; spinal cord	骨髓；脊髓
myring-	tympanic membrane (ear drum)	鼓膜
nephr(o)-	kidney	腎臟
neur	nerve	神經

omo-	shoulder	肩	**pulmo-**	lung	肺
omphalo-	navel	臍	**py(o)-**	pus	膿
oophor-	ovary	卵巢	**pyel-**	pelvis;	骨盆；
opo-	juice	臟腑；血液		kidney pelvis	腎盂
opt-	vision	視覺	**pylor-**	pylorus	幽門
opthalm-	eye	眼睛	**rachio-**	spine	脊柱
orchi-	testicle	睪丸	**rhin-**	nose	鼻
os-	mouth	口腔	**salping-**	tube, especially	管，尤指
ost-	bone	骨		fallopian tube	輸卵管
ot(o)-	ear	耳	**stom(ato)-**	mouth;	口腔；
pharyng-	throat	喉嚨		opening	開口
phleb(o)-	vein	靜脈	**thorac-**	chest	胸部
pleuro-	breast	胸膜	**trache-**	windpipe	氣管
phren-	mind;	精神；意志	**vas-**	vessel	脈管
	midriff	中膈	**vesic-**	bladder	膀胱
pneumo-	lung	肺	**viscer-**	organ, especial-	器官，尤
proct-	anus; rectum	肛門；直腸		ly abdominal	指腹部的

必背醫護相關字首

a(n)-	without; not	無；不	**atreto-**	imperforate	閉鎖、無
ab-	away from;	移去；			孔、不通
	absent	不存在	**auto-**	self	自己、自體
ad-	near; toward	靠近；向	**bacterio-**	bacteria	細菌、菌
ante-	before (time	在(時間或	**balano-**	glans penis	陰頸頭
	or place)	地點)之前	**baro-**	weight	重、壓
anti-	against	抗	**bi-**	two	兩個
archi-	primitive,	原，	**bili-**	bile	膽汁、膽
	beginning	初	**bio-**	life	生活、生命
astro-	star	星(形)	**brachy-**	short	短
atelo-	incomplete	不全			

brady-	slow	緩慢
caco-	bad	不良、惡、有病
caryo-	nucleus, or nut	核
celio-	belly, abdomen	腹， 腹腔
centro-	center	中心，中樞
circum-	around	周圍
contra-	against; opposite	抗； 相反
de-	from, away	除、去、脫、離
deci-	ten	十分之一
demi-	half	一半
di-	two	兩個
dis-	apart	分開
dors(al)-	back	反面
dys-	abnormal; difficult; bad	異常； 困難； 壞
ect(o)-	outside	外面
end-	within	在…之內
epi-	upon	在上、在外
erythr-	red	紅
ex(o)-	away from; outside	遠離； 外面
extra-	beyond	額外
fibro-	fiber	纖維;纖維組織
hemi-	halt	一半
heter(o)-	other	不等,不相似,異
hex(a)-	six	六
hist(o)-	tissue, wed	組織
hemeo-, **hemoeo-**	same, like	相同，相等， 類似
hyper-	above; excessive	在…之上； 超過
hyp(o)-	below; deficient	在…之下； 不足
hypno-	sleep	睡眠、催眠
inter-	between; among	在…之間； 在…之中
intra-	within	在…之內
ischo-	suppress, check	閉止，抑制， 鬱阻
karyo-	nucleus	核
kilo-	a thousand	千
lacto-	milk	乳或乳酸
latero-	side	側或旁
leipo-	to leave, to fail	缺乏， 不足
lepto-	thin	薄,細,小,軟
marco-	large, long	巨，大，長
leuk(o)-	white	白
mal-	ill;bad;poor; abnormal	壞；不良； 異常
mega-	large;huge	大
meno-	menses	月經
meta-	beyond, over, among, after	變化，轉偏， 後，旁，次
mono-	single, one	一個，單一
myxo-	mucus	黏液

narco-	stupor, numbness	麻醉，麻木，昏迷
necr(o)-	corpse; dead tissue	屍體；壞死組織
neo-	new	新
non-	not	不、非
noso-	disease	疾病
ob-	against, in front of, on, toward	抗，在前，在上，向等
octo-	eight	八
olig-	small; few	小；少
ortho-	straight, right	直，正，正常
pachy-	thick	厚，肥，粗
path-	disease	疾病
pent(a)-	five	五
peri-	around	周邊
platy-	broad	濶，扁平
pleo-	more	更多，增多
polio-	gray	灰質，灰色
poly-	many; much	多
post-	after	後，之後
pre-	before	前，之前
pro-	in front of; forward	前面；向前
psycho-	mind, soul	精神，心理
pyr-	fire; heat	火；熱
pyreto-	fever	發熱，熱
re-	again	再，復，反，回
retro-	backward; behind	向後；在…之後
semi-	half	一半
sero-		血清；漿液
sinu-		竇
spiro-	to breathe	呼吸
sten-	narrow; contracted	狹窄；收縮
supra-	above; beyond	在…之上；超過
tachy-	rapid; fast; swift	快速；即時的
trans-	over; across	穿越；橫過

必背醫護相關字尾

Suffix	English	中文
-algia	pain	痛
-ase		酵素，酶
-asthenia	weakness	虛弱
-cele	tumor; hernia; swelling	腫瘤；疝氣；腫脹
-centesis	tapping; puncture	穿刺；放液
-cid(e)	cut; kill	切割；致死
-ectomy	cutting out; excision	切除法；切開
-emia	blood	血液病
-geusia	taste	味
-graph	to record	描記器，檢查器，圖
-iasis	disease condition	病態
-itis	inflammation of	發炎
-lysis	breaking down	瓦解；崩潰
-oid	like	像
-oma	tumor; swelling	瘤；腫
-opia	eye	眼；視力
-oscopy	examination	檢查
-ose		醣類
-osis	disease condition; chronic; increased	疾病狀況；慢性的
-ostomy	a mouth; surgical opening	開口；手術切口
-otomy	incision into	切開
-pathy	disease; suffering	疾病；痛苦
-penia	deficiency; decrease	缺陷；減少
-phobia	persistent abnormal fear	恐…症
-plasty	repair; surgical correction	修復；手術矯正
-plegia	paralysis	痲痺
-pnea	breathing	呼吸
-ptosis	falling; downward; displacement	落下；向下移動
-rhagia	blood flowing	出血
-rhaphy	suture	縫合術
-rhea	flow, discharge	流出；分泌
-uria	condition of urine	尿液的狀況

護士英語會話

編　　著／卓美玲
發行所／學習出版有限公司　☎ (02) 2704-5525
郵撥帳號／0512727-2 學習出版社帳戶
登記證／局版台業 *2179* 號
印刷所／裕強彩色印刷有限公司
台北門市／台北市許昌街 10 號 2 F　☎ (02) 2331-4060
台灣總經銷／紅螞蟻圖書有限公司　☎ (02) 2795-3656
美國總經銷／Evergreen Book Store　☎ (818) 2813622
本公司網址　www.learnbook.com.tw
電子郵件　learnbook@learnbook.com.tw

售價：新台幣一百五十元正

2013 年 9 月 1 日新修訂

ISBN 957-519-159-5